Planet Fashion

Kelly McKain

My
totally secret
journal
by
Lucy Jessica Hartley

Wednesday the 19th of October at 6.06 p.m.

Hey, girls! Lucy Jessica Hartley is back!

I'm starting this journal with my cool new fluffy pen, 'cos I have some amazing info to tell you. You know how your **BFF** (i.e. Best Friends Forever – which is what me and Jules and Tilda call ourselves) are the most cool and fab **VIP**eople in the world? And you know how you usually tend to think you know everything about them 'cos of all the telling secrets you do round the little doorway at the back of the art room (or wherever it is you guys hang out)? Well, I had the most incredible **REVELATION** today that I didn't know this one big thing about Tilda.

Just in case you don't know this, Miss Fabby Tilda Van der Zwan has been **BFF** with me and Jules since she came to our school as a shy new

5

girl. I gave her a makeover to turn her into a groovy babe and now we are totally a three.

We go round together all the time and when we can we link arms to show our **BFF**ness (this is sometimes difficult, like when you're walking down the street in town and a big double pushchair is coming towards you, or when you're trying to all squash through the door of the girls' toilets at once). One of our hobbies is going into the loos at breaktimes to try out different make-up looks in the mirrors. Unfortunately, they don't have any power points in there for hair straighteners so we can't really do total transformations, especially not while wearing our gross-o-matic school uniforms, which are this vile green colour that I reckon was invented just to make school kids look horrible for, like, ~~61%~~ ~~57%~~ ~~62%~~ 5 days of the week! Anyway, I am going off the point. (If you have read my other journals you will probably have already noticed I do that a lot, **BTW**!) (And you will probably also have noticed that I like to write **BTW** a lot, too, which you probably already know means By The Way, **BTW**!)

So anyway, going back to the point, I have found out something about Tilda that made me think, *Oh, maybe I do not know absolutely everything about my BFF like I thought, and maybe Tilda has a secret mysterious side that I didn't know about.*

I can't possibly imagine having a secretly mysterious side myself, even though that would be cool, 'cos I always have to tell everyone everything, like, *straight away.*

Oh, dratification! Mum is calling me down for tea when I have only just started telling you about the secret mysteriosity! I promise to eat fast and carry on writing in here as soon as poss.

It is now after tea,

which was fish fingers, beans and chips – YUM!

Okay, so this is how the secret mysterious thing about Tilda was revealed. Jules was meant to be coming round mine after school like she normally does on Wednesdays 'cos of her dad being at work and her mum taking her little brother and sister (called Benito and Benita – cute or what?!) to Junior Karate and her older bro JJ having his guitar lesson. (BTW, JJ is not my *HSURC TERCES* any more since fancying him caused a giant attack of CRINGITIS to happen to me when he was a model in my fashion show I put on in aid of charity. In fact, right now I don't have a *HSURC TERCES* at all – how unusual for me!)

But anyway, today Jules couldn't come round here 'cos of Mum not being home in time. The reason she was late was 'cos she has recently

8

decided to *Grab Life With Both Hands* as they
say on TV shows,
like this:

She's left her job working for Mr. Snellerman the
Prehistoric Idiot, who thinks she should just
make the tea because of being a woman. I mean,
like, duh, hasn't he ever heard of feministic girl
power? *Everyone* knows it started off with some
women chaining themselves to a railing in
Victorian times and ended up with groovy chicks
marching around professionalistically in clackety
heels running massive companies. Now Mum has
got this part-time job in a cool little shop in

Sherborne which sells cards and mugs and really expensive soap and stuff. She's only working there while she's retraining for a fabulicious career as…

(Drum roll, please!!!)

…a make-up artist!!!

(I know! How cool is that?!)

So she was at her make-up course today in Bristol and she got stuck in traffic on the way home so she asked Mr. Van der Zwan to look after me and Jules, and that's why we ended up not at mine but at Tilda's where we have *never* hung out before.

I know you are right now thinking, *But, Lucy, how come you have never hung out there*

before seeing as Tilda is your BFF? Okay, well, let me explain.

We have never hung round there before (i.e. not even once!) 'cos Tilda doesn't offer and me and Jules don't ask any more, 'cos she always has some reason why we can't. I never really minded anyway 'cos her dad is quite stricty and I thought we wouldn't be able to make **ANY** noise or have **ANY** fun (and there is definitely no Coke or crisps 'cos Tilda isn't usually allowed them).

Even though Tilda lives in a farmhouse, her dad isn't a farmer, but instead he is, well, erm, I don't exactly know, but most of the time he works from home, and then some days he has to go up to The London Office, so it's probably something businessy and important. Tilda and her dad just live together as a two because her mum died when she was very little. Sometimes when I think about that it makes me want to cry 'cos I feel so sorry for Tilda. I just can't imagine what I'd do without my mum, even if she doesn't always *get* me, like when she won't let me use her Shine and Strength Hair Serum just because it's £14.99 per tube, even when I have *frizz*.

When we got to Tilda's, her dad went back up to his study and Tilda got some OJ for us, and these cereal bars with white chocolate on (I was thinking, *Maybe I can just eat the topping and leave the stuck-together-muesli bit*).

Jules said, "Shall we go up to your room?" but Tilda was like, "Oh, actually, do you mind if we go in the sitting room instead and watch this show I like?" So we did and Tilda put the TV on and we all squashed together on one of her posh uprighty sofas.

I know I haven't got to the Mysterious Secret about Tilda yet, but I hope you will manage to put up with me while I just quickly mention something else that happened before the Mysterious Secret was revealed.

Well, the show Tilda liked turned out to be this one called *Go Green!* that is about looking after the planet and becoming more environmental by recycling your old cans and newspapers and switching off lights and growing some veggies in your garden so you don't have to buy ones from New Zealand or wherever.

Anyway, the presenter on *Go Green!* is a girl called Aisha, who's on lots of different programmes. She's really cool and has a great sense of fashion and style (which, as you know, is of v. v. massivo interest to me 'cos being a *Real Actual Fashion Designer* is my life's ambition). So we were watching this show and Jules was poking my foot with her foot and I was poking her foot back and scraping the white chocolate topping

13

off the cereal bar with my teeth (and starting to think how I might have been tricked and how it did in fact not taste like white chocolate but more like *yogurt* that they have somehow made solid)... so basically we were not concentrating that much on the programme.

There was this bit though where these kids were in the studio with Aisha talking about this recycling system they had made for their school. That was when I started having an all-out foot war with Jules and we fell off the uprighty sofa, but anyway, after the recycling kids went off, Aisha looked at us and said, "Do you want to be on TV?"

Jules stopped lying on the floor with her feet pummelling me and sat up straight, yelling, "Yes, we do!"

I nearly choked on my suspiciously-not-white-chocolate-coated cereal bar with sudden concentration, because being on TV would be completely amazing and cool beans. So then us three were all just staring at Aisha. She said,

14

"E-mail us with details of *your* green project and, you never know, we might invite you onto the show!"

Even though she was just saying it generally to the public, it felt as if she knew exactly what we were thinking and like she had said,

If you, Lucy, Jules and Tilda, have a cool idea for a green project, I want to hear specifically from you three!

"We are *soooooo* going in for that!" ~~said~~ ~~squealed~~ ~~shouted~~ exclaimed Jules.

BTW, I like the idea of people exclaiming stuff - it makes it sound like we are in a book. I'm going to put that more often!

Then Jules exclaimed more stuff, like, "If I can get on telly maybe someone will notice my talent and then I'll star in a movie and go to Hollywood and be famous!" Of course, as you know, Jules wants to be an actress, and she is definitely very dramatic 'cos of being all Spanishly fiery and passionate, so she should be fab at it!

Tilda said, "It would be fun to do a green project, and good for the planet, and I don't even mind if we don't get chosen to go on the TV show."

Then they both looked at me.

They had to wait while I dislodged the muesli bits from down my throat by gargling my orange juice, but then I went, "Yeah, it would be totally amazing to help the planet *and* get on TV. We just need to think of a green project."

After I said that they were both still looking at me, in this way of like *expecting* me to say something. And that's when I realized they thought I was about to come up with an amazing idea that actual second. I checked my brain for *Creative*

Inspirations but none were there, and Jules and Tilda didn't have any either.

But at that very moment I got distracted from thinking about green project ideas, because that's when I found out the Mysterious Secret about Tilda. I had to go upstairs to the loo and while I was there I spent ages trying out different smiles in the mirror 'cos I think it's time I had a new one. The one I have now is all teeth and it makes me look like an insane crazy person. I have been sketching smiles on Post-its all day. Oh, hang on, I will stick them in here.

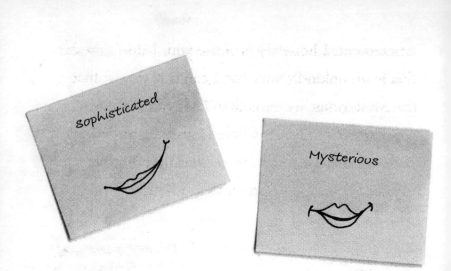

It's tricky 'cos I need one that I can use for smiling at cool boys in the corridor at school, but that also works for smiling in class so it looks like I know the answer when I don't. I am working on a cross between the sophisticated and mysterious ones at the moment.

Anyway, when I came out of the loo I was so busy practising my smiles while walking along that instead of going down the stairs I walked past them and turned into a doorway by accident.

And then I was just standing there in horrified

amazement. I honestly promise you, I don't mean this in an unkindly way, but I can now reveal that the Mysterious Secret is that Tilda has **THE** most ungroovy room in the whole history of really yucky bedroom design and I feel *extreeeeeemely* sorry for her for having to live in it! It looks like this:

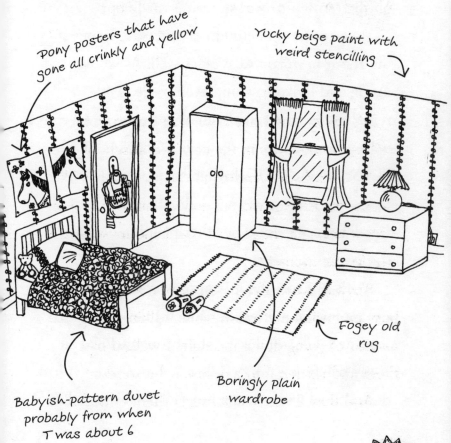

Pony posters that have gone all crinkly and yellow

Yucky beige paint with weird stencilling

Babyish-pattern duvet probably from when I was about 6

Boringly plain wardrobe

Fogey old rug

I tried to pull my eyes away, but unfortunately I am the nosiest person on this planet of Earth so I was still staring when Tilda came dashing up the stairs. "Oh, Lucy!" she cried. "You weren't supposed to see in there!" Her cheeks had gone the colour of tomato soup, which is about an eight on the *Cringe-o-meter* scale I made up.

Jules came up behind her and was staring at the room in *utter horror* as well. As we went inside and looked around even more, Tilda revealed that she actually made sure we never came up here *on purpose*. I was in GOBSMACKED FLABBERGASTATION when she said that, 'cos that's like for a *year*, and I didn't notice – maybe I really am *oblivious* to other people as Mum sometimes says I am.

"It's not too bad," I started saying.

"At least it's original," added Jules.

But Tilda could see right through us like an X-ray machine. "I hate it too!" she wailed. "It just doesn't feel like *me* any more! That's why I didn't want you to come up here, 'cos *your* rooms are so cool and I thought you'd think mine was so hideously repulsive that maybe you wouldn't want to be my **BFF** any more!"

We gave her a big hug then.

"Oh, Tilda, of course we don't care what your room looks like!" I said.

"Even if you lived in a shed decorated with mouldy broccoli and pigeon poo we would still love you 'cos you're our **BFF**," added Jules.

"Thanks," said Tilda. "Sorry I even thought that – I should have known you are true **BFF**. I have to do something about this awful room, though. I really want to redecorate, but Dad's always too busy to help me and I don't know where to start on my own. I don't even know what kind of look I *want*." She threw her hands in the air in a gesture of desperateness, and that's when I realized that our **BFF** needed serious help, and that *we* were the ones to give it to her!

"We can help you!" I said, feeling mega-ly

excited. "We can completely redo it and turn it into a cool girly den!"

"That's so nice of you, Lu," said Tilda, but she was still looking glumly gloomy. "The problem is that Dad's busy on some international merger thingamabob that's got to be all sorted out within the next two weeks. There's no way he'll have time to help and I know he won't let us go ahead unless we have *adult supervision*."

We all thought for a bit about how we could get *adult supervision*. I know Mum is also too busy to help us 'cos of her new course. Jules didn't say anything, so I guess her parents are, too, and my Nan (who likes to be called Delia, **BTW**) is away visiting Great Auntie Rita. So it seemed like there was no one to help and that the room would have to stay awful. But then I had the **REVELATION** that my *dad* is an adult! I didn't think of him before because, as Mum likes to say, he doesn't exactly act like one. (**BTW**, Mum and Dad split up about a year ago and it was really hard for me and my little bro Alex 'cos they were still rowing all the time even though they were not living together. They have started being sort of friends now, though.) I told Jules and Tilda I'd ask him, and I was pretty sure he'd say yes, 'cos his DJing job's at night so in the daytime he is normally just sleeping and watching MTV and strumming his guitar while watching his pants dry on the radiator in my Uncle Ken's flat, which is where he now lives.

So I called Dad and he did say yes (yay!) and then we went to ask Tilda's dad. Tilda knocked on his study door and me and Jules were like, *gulp*, in case he was stricty at us for disturbing him, but actually he was really nice. He said, "I'm so sorry I can't help you girls myself, because of my Big Important Work Project that I have on." (*BTW*, he didn't in fact say Big Important Work Project, but you get what I mean.) Anyway, then he was also like, "But if your dad is happy to supervise, Lucy, then it's fine for you girls to go ahead. I can pay for the paint and other things you'll need. Actually, this will be a good learning experience for you and a worthwhile exercise in money management."

Then he told Tilda how much budget we could have and it was so minuscule that it will be more like an exercise in money *magic* to do a whole room out of that! But now I am thinking that in fact having no money just means we have to be more creative with thinking of ideas for furniture and decorations, so it's probably okay.

After asking, we went back into Tilda's room and I instantly started having *Creative Inspirations* about what we could do, like making picture frames and gluing beads on them, and having Indian sarongs for the curtains (Tilda loved that idea). Plus Jules said about putting up fairy lights and how we would need to get a new wardrobe and chest of drawers instead of the yucky old pine ones.

Tilda was like, "On our budget?" and then for one minute we were a bit sad 'cos if there are those two hulking great bits of disgustingness still in the room it will ruin the whole cool effect.

Then suddenly I remembered something from this room design show that I was sort of watching 'cos Mum had it on when she was painting my toenails the other day in this cool shade called Cherry Bomb. "I know, if we get some paint and water it down and sort of rub it over the wood, it makes it go all groovy," I told them. "So it will be the same furniture but different, as in no longer disgusting, but cool-looking."

Tilda smiled. "Good thinking," she said. "I like the idea of reusing stuff we've already got, and I really want to use eco-friendly paints without the nasty chemicals in."

"How about purple and black for the paints?" said Jules all excitedly, 'cos of her being a *Goth Rock Chick*.

"Maybe purple and something else apart from black," said Tilda thoughtfully, and then they started getting all excited talking about colours.

Meanwhile I was standing in utter stillness and silencio, with my brain ticking like a giant clock, like maybe even Big Ben or something.

Suddenly I went, "Hey!" really loud and they turned round and stared at me. "You do know what this is, don't you?" I said, waving my arms at Tilda's room.

Jules put her hands on her hips and sighed. "Yes, Lucy, it's a horrible bedroom that we are going to change into a cool girly den," she said. She was *soooooo* not getting me.

So I was like, "No. Well, *yes*, but also, it's a green project! We can send this idea in to the TV show!"

They both stared at me for a moment and then this invisible light bulb went on above Jules's head like she *had* got it and Tilda cried, "Of course!" and they both swamped me in a big **BFF** hug.

We all got totally excited then — if it was a musical we would have danced around singing about all the stuff we could do, but it was Real Life so we obviously didn't. When we started looking at the whole room again we realized that we could make *everything* green by reusing it, repainting it, recycling it or refurbishing it (which is interior-design language for doing it up to look nice, BTW). That way we're not buying new things and also we're not wasting old things. Genius, *n'est-ce pas?*

So then we were having loads of *Creative Inspirations*, like Jules was going, "We can use the environmentally friendly paint that Tilda was saying about," and Tilda was going, "And even if we do have to buy some things we could make them as green as possible, by buying second-hand," and I added, "Yeah, or getting things made by local people so they have not flown gazillions of miles like my fave apples, and we could even have stuff made out of recycled other stuff, like this lamp Mum's friend Gloria's got that used to be a wine bottle."

Tonight, Tilda is e-mailing the *Go Green!* show to explain about our idea (she even took some pix with her dad's digital camera to send in, to show exactly how disgusting the room is and what a hard challenge it will be!). I really, *really* hope they pick our project to go on the show! Ideally, I would keep all my fingers crossed till we hear back, but in actuality that will be way too difficult, what with having to do my eyeshadow and us pouring chemical-y stuff into test tubes in science and that.

Of course, the second I got home I told Mum all about it and so now she is keeping everything crossed for me too (as in the saying – not as in she is walking round like a game of Twister gone wrong).

Oh, hang on, talking of Mum, she has just called me to come down and put all the clean socks in pairs for her. That is one of the things

I have to do for my pocket money, and 'cos I have my eye on this mood-change ring in Claire's Accessories I have to make sure I tick off all my jobs this week or I won't get my £5. I don't mind doing Mum's and my socks, but I **HATE** doing Alex's 'cos even when they have only just been in the wash, I'm sure they still have a little bit of the smell of yucky boy's feet on them.

Urgh! I bet *Real Actual Fashion Designers* don't have to put their little bro's smelly socks into pairs! They are probably way too busy sitting in glam clubs drinking cool fruit cocktails with little umbrellas in. Still, I can check what washing powder we have while I'm there and see if it is eco-friendly.

It is 8 o'clock-ish

and the socks are all in twos, BTW.

Tilda just texted me to say she sent our green-a-licious project idea off to the TV show – yay! So now I am totally on *tenterhooks* (still don't know what they are, BTW!) hoping that we'll get picked! I wonder how long it will take for them to reply?!

Seeing as I am now the *Goddess of Green*, I have decided that we have to get more environmental at home, so I went round turning

off the lights to save electricity. Mum was actually trying to read a mag in the living room at the time, though, and she made me switch them back on again.

I did mention to her that she is destroying the planet, but she said, "Until we get mandatory targets for reducing CO_2 emissions in the Bali agreement, I don't suppose me reading

Celeb mag under
a 40-watt bulb is going to
make much difference, Lu."
But she is in fact wrong 'cos
if we all do our bit then it
will make a massivo difference.
Right, I am off to have a bath.

8.42 o'clock

FYI, environmental baths are not that fun. Because
of saving water, it's more like lying in a warm
puddle, which is not something that anyone would
decide to do out of their own choice. Oh well, I
will just have to change to showers from now on.

Thursday at first break

We are in the little doorway round the back of the art room.

There isn't much space in here so we're squashed up together and it is all elbows. Tilda checked her e-mail before school this morning but there's nothing from the *Go Green!* people yet. Hopefully when she goes on tonight there will be a message saying, *Yes, yes, yes, please come on our TV show IMMEDIATELY with your ultra-groovy green project!*

I am in charge of writing down ideas for the room makeover, like what sort of stuff Tilda wants and what we need to do. I am doing a list like a proper interior designer would, with different categories and underlining and stuff.

<u>Project:</u> Give Tilda's bedroom a green makeover.

<u>Style:</u> Hippy-type stuff but in a "cool and groovy

girl" type way and not a "smelly old caravan" type way.

Colours: Tilda likes purple the most, and also yellow and she just said she would like some spangly sequinny bits somewhere too.

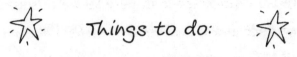 Things to do:

1. Paint the walls – so we need to buy paint testers. Jules suggested that we could choose different colours for each of the walls but I'm not too sure about that. Maybe we could have a different colour for the skirting-boardy thing and the door, though, apart from just boring old white.

2. Mirror – i.e. get one from somewhere (a charity shop?) and decorate it so we can make Tilda a dressing table by propping it up on her chest of drawers.

3. Lamp – find out where Gloria got that wine-bottle one from.

4. Rug. Tilda has got sanded-down floorboards that are at this moment mainly hidden by a horrible rug. (**BTW**, Tilda just *told* me to write "horrible" — that is not me being horrible by writing "horrible" myself!) We have no idea how you could make one or get a recycled one. Maybe we can try looking it up on the net

That was Jules accidentally jogging me!

5. Some sort of chairs or beanbags or something to make a cool chill-out zone.

6. Curtains or blinds that are somehow reused or made of some eco-friendly material. Tilda still likes the idea of sari ones, so I will have to work out where to get some from.

7. Painting the furniture like we said.

Oh typical, the bell is ringing. Why is it that just when we are doing something massively vital, school gets in the way?

I am at home now, BTW

We had a few more ideas for the room makeover during lessons, so at least we did get something useful done. I mean, it is not exactly that vital to know about the Chartist Movement or Peristalsis

BOOM! when we are facing *Imminent Environmental Destruction*, is it? I'm just sticking them in here in case they get lost.

Jules just realized we need to think of cushions and a different duvet or bedspread or something. Just wanted to write that down quickly before I forget!

How about a sort of chandelier twinkly light shade with purple beads on?

Tilda says what pictures or posters should we have? 'Cos those pony ones will have to go!

When I got in just now Mum asked me to help with getting the dinner and I said how I am too busy saving the planet. Then I told her about our new ideas for the green room makeover and I asked her if I could give Tilda my purple duvet set, 'cos then hers would be recycled and plus then I could get that Groovy Chick one I saw in the Argos catalogue. But she said, "I'm afraid not, Lucy. You don't need a new duvet set. And besides, money doesn't grow on trees."

I said, "Well, in fact, it kind of does because money is paper and paper comes from wood and wood comes from trees."

Mum leaned back against the kitchen counter and did her eyebrow-raising thing which means she is not going to put up with any of my nonsense, and said, "If you've got time to be a cheeky madam you've got time to help me with the dinner." So I am only supposed to be up here changing and washing my hands, 'cos now I have to go and peel carrots!

The good news is that Mum is letting us have this old mirror that's in the loft for Tilda's room. It's got a gold-coloured frame with all curly bits on, like this:

I think if we paint it white or light purple (I mean the frame obviously, not the actual glass bit!), then I could glue some beads to it, and maybe we could even get a feather boa to put round it as well. It would look fab hung on the wall above Tilda's chest of drawers, making a cool girly dressing table where she can put all her make-up and nail polish and spangly hairgrips, instead of having them in an old Sainsbury's bag hanging from the back of her door like she does at the moment!

Mum said after tea she'll show me this new thing she learned at college about layering on different shades of natural-coloured eyeshadow to change your eye shape. It is *sooooo* cool that she's going to be a make-up artist! I can hardly wait till she's finished her training and she's jetting off to do Kate Moss's make-up for New York Fashion Week and stuff like that. Maybe if I'm a *Perfect Daughter* she'll let me go along with her. I guess I'd better start being one by peeling those carrots, then!

Oh, I know, I can save the peelings for compost, which we can use to grow new carrots in, so we will have new carrots out of old carrots instead of out of Sainsbury's – how green is that?! (Or should that be *how orange?!*)

Friday,

at the end of lunchtime –
no word from the TV people
this morning either (boo!)
but it is the last day of school
before half-term today (yay!).

I am in the girls' loos writing this – not
sitting on the actual loo but just on the
closed seat of the loo, so don't worry, there
is nothing toilet-ish happening. I have just
come straight from the computer room
(which is why I don't have my journal on
me, which explains why I am having to write
this on loo paper) – I know you are thinking,
But Lucy why would you possibly go there?
Well, the reason is that Jules is at drama
club and Tilda has her piano lesson so I said
I'd go and look on the web to try and find
out about eco-friendly rugs and any other

cool green stuff we might need.

So I got to the computer room and Simon Driscott was there, of course, 'cos of computers being his fave thing ever. He virtually lives in there, which explains why he is so pale and pasty. (BTW, Simon Driscott is this boy who I used to call the Prince of Pillockdom but who I have recently found out is quite funny and okay, so now he is my sort of friend, but with no fancying going on whatsoever.) Him and the ~~Geeky Minions~~ whoops, I mean his Charming Friends are ~~computer geeks~~ whoops, I mean computer geniuses. I am trying to be nicer to them since they helped me with the lighting and sound engineering for my charity fashion show. Anyway, when I went in they were all completely glued to the computers playing medieval battle games.

Simon looked up and exclaimed, "Noble knights,

here cometh a fair maiden into our encampment!"

I was thinking, Noble knights? Yeah right!
The Geeky Minions are so weedy that if you
charged at any of them with a real sword in
actual life they'd just run away screaming and
hide under a bed, like:

Non-noble
knights

When I walked by them, the GMs all
automatically hunched over the computers and
looked even more interested in the medieval-
battley game.

"Oh, come on, please let me have a go on a computer, it's important," I said to Simon.

"I suppose you have to check that peach lipstick is still in vogue since yesterday," he said, smirkingly. (Like, ha ha, he is soooooo funny.)

"I have to save the planet actually, NOT that it's any of your business," I said back, before adding, "and, duh, no one wears peach lipstick any more now that there is Sheer Shine Glide-On Very Berry Juicy Jelly lipgloss."

Simon just did that annoying smirking thing again as if something is funny when nothing is. I sat in this swivel chair right next to him and swivelled round and round annoyingly until he couldn't concentrate on shooting arrows. He sighed and let his little computer knight person get run over by a horse and then went, "What can I do for you, Lucy?" He asked it in this way like he is completely in charge of the computer room his actual self, which he so isn't.

"I need to find out about green things," I said.

"Cucumbers, trees, limes? You'll have to be a bit more specific," he went, just to be annoying 'cos of course he knew what I meant.

I did my You-are-such-an-idiot-it-is-not-worth-me-even-bothering-to-reply face, and he went, "Just a second. I'll get Google up."

But his silly comment about green-ness had made me annoyed so I said, "No, I'll be fine on my own thanks ACTUALLY." Then I used my swivel chair like a dodgem to shove him out of the way of the computer screen, and he tried to stay there by hanging on to the edge of the desk and we had a sort of swivel-chair fight which was actually really fun until I accidentally banged my wrist. I pretended it hurt a bit more than it did so that Simon had to be nice to me and let me have the computer.

Then I typed "green ideas" into Google and

44

I got this massive list of weird stuff which didn't seem to be anything to do with room design. So I did in fact need Simon to help me (but I pretended it was only 'cos I couldn't type with my sore wrist, so he didn't think I am completely an incapable idiot about technologicality).

We found loads of cool stuff in the end. I didn't print any of it out because of trying to save paper, but I can squeeze in some pix here if I draw them quite small.

Energy-saving light bulbs

Organic cotton bedspread

Cool cushion

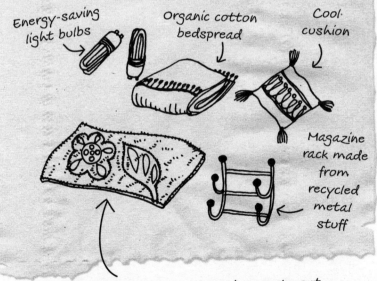

Magazine rack made from recycled metal stuff

BTW, we found these cool rugs that they make out of old plastic bags in Cornwall. They don't sound that nice, but they look really, really cool! I e-mailed the link to Tilda so if she likes them she can ask her dad about ordering one.

Friday still,
but at 8.16 p.m.

Tilda just texted me **AGAIN** to say there is **STILL** nothing from the TV people, even though she has checked 17 times in the last 4 hours. Our idea is *soooooo* cool I don't get why they haven't replied back straight away! Oh well, at least T loves the old-plastic-bags rug and she is asking her dad about getting one!

Saturday,
at Tilda's house,
where we are putting the
Great Green Makeover Plan
into action.

I am just quickly writing this while Tilda and
Jules are making us some sandwiches, to tell you
what's happened so far. I don't reckon the TV
people will e-mail today because of work being on
weekdays only for office-y people, so I will have
to try and control my hopingness till Monday.

Anyway, you know how my dad is usually a
bit embarrassing? The thing is, today he was even
more embarrassing than ever, and in front of my
BFF too! He collected me this morning and then
we picked up Jules and Tilda and went to this big
DIY store by the dual carriageway. Dad didn't
have a car for ages and he used to annoy Mum by
asking to borrow ours all the time, but now he is

doing well in his DJ job (which is at our local radio station Wicked FM) he has bought one.

It's this cool sports car with only a tiny back seat that Jules and Tilda had to squash into. It's bright red and he had the top down 'cos it was a nice day and we all had our sunglasses on. I felt *soooooo* cool for about 2.5 seconds, until Dad spoiled the vibe by calling the car "she", as in, "When I get her on the open road, Lu, she really flies! Keeping her on top form is very satisfying for a *motor enthusiast* like me."

I said, "Oh, so it's not like you're having a Midlife Crisis or anything, which is what Mum reckoned when you pulled up this morning."

Dad went, "How witty of her!" and did a fake laugh while grinding the gears by accident.

We went in the paint part of the DIY store and Dad managed to be completely embarrassing by thinking he is a total DIY expert when he is *soooooo NOT.*

This is what happened ⟶

1. This wallpaper-removing machine was just being on display, minding its own business.
2. Dad decided to act all expert and give us a demonstration of how to use it.

3. Dad broke the machine in a really **LOUD** way.
4. **EVERYONE** stared at us.
5. Dad walked quickly away from it, while Jules and Tilda tried not to laugh.
6. I had a giant attack of **CRINGITIS!!!**

While I was busy wishing I could dig a hole in the ground with the Eas-e-drill (also on display) and disappear into it, Dad went *hurrumph hurrumph* in a clearing-his-throat way and said, "Right, let's get on with choosing this paint then." He was limping a bit because the heavy end of the wallpaper-remover thingie had fallen on his foot.

Me and Jules and Tilda picked loads of different purples and yellows in sample-size pots, and we were really excited about getting back to Tilda's to try them out.

When he let us in, Mr. Van der Zwan offered Dad a drink, but Dad said no thanks and zoomed off really quickly, making the gravel in the drive whoosh up in a show-offy way. He's popping home for lunch and then coming back later with all the other painting equipment and big pots of the colours (after we have chosen our final ones and rung him back to say what they are, of course).

Oh, Jules and Tilda are calling me to come for my sandwich. I hope it's made of local produce that hasn't been flown here from across the world!

Saturday at 5.32 p.m.

I am lying on my bed recovering from all the hard work we did today and eating a green apple (i.e. it is green as in green-coloured, and also green as in planet-friendly 'cos it is from Dorset. I know it is from Dorset 'cos I got it off the tree in our garden. I actually wanted a Wagon Wheel but they are probably flown here all the way from cowboy ranches in the Wild West of America, so I resisted.

We had such a cool time today doing the room makeover! There is loads to tell you but I am totally whacked out from all the painting so I will try to say it quickly (tricky for me!). Also, I have to work out how to get purple paint out of my hair (lucky it's half-term next week 'cos if Mr. Cain saw it he would think I dyed it on purpose and go completely mad with a capital M, as in

51

Mad. **BTW**, Mr. Cain is this teacher at school who is totally like my arch-enemy 'cos he is the *School Uniform Police* and I am a *Style Guru!*)

Before we even so much as opened the lid off one tester, Tilda's dad gave us these big unfunky painting shirts to wear. They were his old work ones and completely ginormous and they looked awful. So I had to do a five-minute emergency makeover on us to turn them cool.

AFTER

BEFORE

Oh whoops, I forgot to tell you about the paints we chose earlier. The testers we got were:

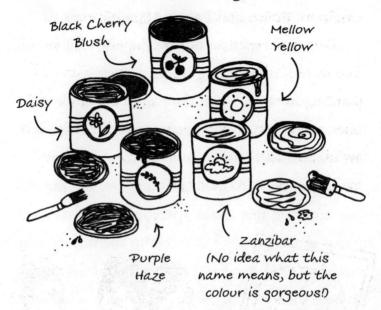

Black Cherry Blush

Mellow Yellow

Daisy

Purple Haze

Zanzibar (No idea what this name means, but the colour is gorgeous!)

We painted the colours onto some white art paper and then Blu-tacked them up in a line. We stood back and inspected them and had a really good time shuffling them round and trying different ones out next to each other. Black Cherry Blush should have been called Yucky Mush 'cos it came out this weird muddy brown colour, but we totally loved Zanzibar, which is this hippyish yellow that's actually much more mellow than the Mellow Yellow, which is actually really bright. In the end we decided to go for Purple Haze on most of the walls, and to put Zanzibar on the one wall behind Tilda's bed to make a groovy contrast.

We rang Dad about the paint, and while we were waiting for him to come back, us three got on with clearing the room out. We packed all Tilda's books and desk stuff in boxes and put her soft toys and that in the spare room and took down her posters. Then we covered up the furniture with old sheets. We made up this game of billowing up a sheet then running under it and it was like being inside a giant white cloud. Then we all rolled around in it pretending to be mummies (i.e. the Egyptian kind!) and got into utter hysterics. So by the time Dad came back we could hardly even get one sentence out we were laughing so much.

I wanted to just start painting the walls straight away but according to Dad it is *Not That simple*. First you have to do all this boring stuff like filling in any holes and washing the whole lot down with water that has a tiny bit of washing-up liquid squeezed in. Dad had this massive tool belt on, and all these things like electric drills and weird hammers in a tool box, which he didn't really need, but obviously they made him feel manly and show-offy to Mr. Van der Zwan!

After about one hour, Mr. VDZ came in to ask Dad if he wanted a coffee (and plus he said Dad should help himself to drinks in future in case he is too busy on his Vital Project of Business-ness or whatever it is). When he came back with the coffee he brought us **BFF** some lemon squash without even checking what *we* wanted – in fact I fancied coffee too, but Tilda's dad still doesn't get that we are not little kids but *very actual teenagers* so I didn't mention anything.

It was about 4 p.m. when we finally started the actual painting. We all clapped when Tilda put the first big stripe of Purple Haze on the wall. As we carried on it was so cool to see the horrible colour

(in its pot it was probably called Hideous Beige!)
disappear under the lovely purple. We had the
radio on and we were singing along to all the cool
songs like Jess Moon's and that. Plus, we found
this way of dancing while still painting the room,
by wiggling our hips and stepping back and
forward away from the wall. We all got in time
with each other and it was so funny.

Dad joined in with the singing and I was
thinking *yikes!* and trying to make my ears
extendable out of the window to avoid the terrible
racket, like:

But then I noticed he was kind of okay and I thought how it was actually quite cool to have a dad who messes around with you (although I'm not telling *him* that, of course!).

When Mum came to get me she had a look at the room and said what a good job we are doing, even Dad. She teased him about some of the filler not being even and he was like, "It's meant to be like that, *actually*, Sue, and **FYI** I've always been a *motor enthusiast* so it's perfectly normal that I would get an MGB convertible in Vermilion Red, seeing as I have always wanted one but *you* would never let me."

Mum looked at me and I looked at the empty Purple Haze tin while thinking, *Whoops, maybe I shouldn't have mentioned her comment about Dad actually to him.* I was worried they would start having one of their massive arguments again, but luckily Mum just smiled at him and was all nice, saying, "Well, anyway, Brian, it's very kind of you to help the girls like this."

Dad looked mega-ly surprised but quite pleased when she said that.

I don't mind them being separated as much now that they are getting on better, 'cos me and Alex still get to see Dad a lot, but Mum and Dad are both more happy as well. I'm also glad that neither of them are into meeting anyone new, 'cos after all the upheaval and not-very-nice-ness of them splitting up in the first place I don't want anything else to change!

Just when we were going home Mr. VDZ invited us round for Sunday lunch tomorrow — me, Mum, Dad and Alex, that is. Dad said thanks but how he had stuff to do at the radio station (which I reckon is an excuse 'cos he does a Saturday night show, i.e. tonight, but then he doesn't do another one till Monday) but the rest of the Hartleys are going. How cool is that? I get to spend extra time with Tilda on a family day — hooray! I hope Jules doesn't mind — she'd gone home by then but I know she won't be able to come anyway 'cos her family always go to church on Sunday and then have loads of people round for a big paella.

Oh, speaking of food, I've gotta go 'cos we're having our usual DVD and pizza night tonight and it's my turn 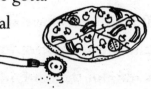 to choose the film. Alex reckons he should get two turns 'cos me and Mum are both girls so he has to watch 66.6% girls' films and only 33.3% boys' films. But I told *him* it has to be one person, one vote, like in democracy, or it's not fair. Mum said, "Wherever did you get the impression that life is fair, Lucy? And by the way, if there's any more loud and embarrassing arguing in the video shop no one will be getting anything."

Charming, n'est-ce pas?

Gotta go!

10.34 p.m.
(annoyingly!)

I can't sleep for some reason (I have been lying here trying since 9.44). Oh, actually, I have just remembered that Dad's radio show is on so I think I'll turn the light off again and put my clock radio on really quietly and listen with my eyes shut.

11.05 p.m.

Eeeeeeekkkkkk!!! I am WIDE AWAKE now!!!

After this one song Dad was chatting to some caller-inners and I was only half listening and then he said, "Let's have some more music now. This one is for Veruschka. I can't wait to see you tomorrow, babe. Let's go for a spin with the top down!" And then he put on this totally smulchy love song. I was sitting bolt upright with my eyes wide open staring in **FLABBERGASTED GOBSMACKEDNESS** at the wall by this point. Who *is* this Veruschka person? Even though I don't know *who* she is I think I know who she *is*, if you get what I mean.

I think she is my dad's girlfriend!

Yikes!

I absolutely and totally cannot believe it!

Well, there's no way I can sleep now! I am just going to have to lie here feeling *shocked* and *horrified* for the whole entire night and possibly the rest of my life! Thanks very much, Dad!

<u>12.09</u>
in the middle of the night.

Oh no, every time I shut my eyes I get this imagination of the Veruschka person, that's like:

Wicked smirk like Cruella de Vil

Cloud of perfume that makes you nearly pass out

Long red nails that can cut through glass

Tiny denim miniskirt

Sharp heels for, like, kicking puppies and stuff

Argh! I am going to have to try sleeping with my eyes *open*. I wonder if that's even possible?!

Sunday afternoon,

sitting at the kitchen table
by the window so I don't
have to put the light on
and waste electricity.

I am back at home after our yummy lunch at
Tilda's. I managed to enjoy it (well, at least to
begin with) even though I am still in shocked
horrification about The Dad Thing.

When we got there Mum was going, "Oh,
Christiaan, how kind of you to invite us." In case
you are thinking, Erm, who? Christiaan is in fact
Mr. Van der Zwan's Christian name (weird, huh?
And yes it is meant to have 2 as). But I can never
call him that 'cos I have called him Mr. Van der
Zwan or Stricty Dad for too long to change now.

Mr. Van der Zwan said that Mum looked lovely
and they did kissing on the cheek which went a bit
wrong 'cos she did one and he did two and caught

63

her on the nose, and they had this embarrassed laugh about it.

Mum of course instantly asked if she could help with the lunch 'cos that is how nice she is, but Mr. VDZ said it was all under control and gave her a glass of wine and told her to relax, so she just sat down at the kitchen table. I said I wasn't thirsty 'cos I didn't want to end up with lemon squash again.

 Mum was going "Ooooooh, it smells delicious" and "Oooooh, you've got a fabulous pan set" and "Ooooooh, I'd love a Neff fan oven like yours, it must be very efficient" and other kitchen-related stuff like that.

Alex the creep offered to help too, so Mr. VDZ gave him the job of stirring the gravy, even though I secretly don't think it actually *needed* stirring.

64

Mr. VDZ also gave Alex a stripey chef's apron the same as his, like:

Mr. VDZ and his mini-me
— reunited at last!

It reminded me of when they had matching embarrassing sandals on holiday and spent the whole time doing nature walks and going birdwatching and that. *shudder!*

Luckily for me all the helping was being done, so I got a chance to slip off upstairs with Tilda.

We were wearing too-nice clothes to carry on

with the painting and also we
didn't want Jules to come back
and see we had done some
without her and feel left out.
But luckily I'd brought my box
of material scraps and beads and

ribbon, etc., for making the plain pink cushions
on Tilda's bed more funky, so we got on with that
instead. This is the design we came up with:

BEFORE

AFTER

Jazzy
sequins

Red
fabric-
paint
flower

Boringly plain
cushion cover

Ribbons
stitched on
in a swirl

Groovy tassles
made from ribbon
with beads on

While we were doing the cushions this kind of quiet concentrationy atmosphere descended and then suddenly we were having this serious girly chat. I **LOVE** serious girly chats, even as much as peach and papaya bubble bath or getting a free gift on the front of my fave mag, *Hey Girls!*

I went, "I was just wondering if, erm, whether…do you ever think about your dad meeting someone else?"

Tilda looked up and she was like, "Weird question – why are you asking?"

I told her about what Dad had said on the radio when I was accidentally listening. I ended up by saying, "Well, it made me think about what if he does really like this Veruschka person and what if by some miracle she really likes him, and what if they get married and what if she turns out to be a horrible wicked stepmother who makes me wear rags and just wash her Tiny Denim Miniskirts all day?" I felt a bit like I couldn't breathe then and I had to concentrate really hard on gluing sequins

67

on the cushion to stop myself panicking.

Tilda took ages to speak. Then finally she said, "When Mum first died I used to worry about stuff like that too, but…" She fiddled with a bit of fabric, making sure it was really properly stuck down even though it already was. "Well, she's been gone so long now and Dad's never been interested in anyone else and he hasn't even had a single date so I don't really worry about it any more."

I kind of wished she did worry about her dad too, 'cos her not worrying about him made me feel all alone with my strange new thoughts about *my* dad. In fact, I was just feeling like I was on my own desert island of miserability when luckily Tilda cheered me up. She rolled up her skirt so it was really tiny and teetered on her tiptoes as if she was wearing really high heels and towered over me doing that waggly finger thing, going,

I am your eeeevil stepmother, Veruschka. Your washing of my Tiny Denim Miniskirts ees not good enough! Do them again, wicked child!

That made me burst out laughing, and also made it seem very unlikely to happen, so I felt much better. After we had stopped giggling, Tilda plonked down on the floor again and said, "But seriously, your dad seems so nice I'm sure he wouldn't start liking someone who was *that* awful."

I said thanks and thought what a cool **BFF** Tilda is. I told her I'm sure the date has gone terribly

anyway, and that the Veruschka person will
most likely be put off by:

A) Dad's manky flat
B) his scary driving
C) his terrible guitar playing

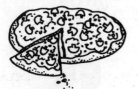

D) him taking her to
somewhere like Pizza Hut
instead of anywhere posh

And actually, even:

E) if he tells just *one* of his awful jokes

That is five different ways for him to be
doomed, so I shouldn't really need to worry.

Just then Mum and Mr. VDZ did a big laugh
both at once in the kitchen and Tilda suddenly
looked up and caught my eye. She gave me this
weird look and out of nowhere she went, "As I
said, there will never be anyone else for my dad
apart from my mum, not even someone really nice,
for example."

I was like, "Sure, you already said that," totally not getting why she'd mentioned it again.

But then when we were all having the Sunday lunch together I…well, I don't want to say this and I *soooooo* don't want to write it down in my beautiful journal, but then I do sort of want to tell you, 'cos it could be a mega-ly important thing. Well, we were all having the delish roast beef and these ginormous Yorkshire puddings and Alex kept going, "I did the gravy" every two minutes, and Mum and Mr. VDZ were still in their laughing mood. Then Tilda said, "Lucy, could you pass the carrots, please?" and I suddenly saw things not as Lucy but as if I was this stranger who had just walked in and didn't know us. I saw what that person would see, which is one family with a mum and dad and two girls and a boy as the children.

Eeeeeeeeeeeeeekkkkkkkkkkk!!!!!

Even *eeeeeeekier*, I also suddenly realized that Tilda might think that *I* think her dad fancies my mum and maybe that's why she said that weird thing when we heard them laughing in the kitchen! And then I was like, what if Mum *does* fancy him? I couldn't have possibly imagined it a couple of months ago, but after we all had the holiday together and with him being such a good cook and everything…

Once I had been struck with these scary thinkings, I had to virtually force my food down my throat while keeping a big smile on my face so that no one would possibly guess what I was thinking. Seriously, I was so freaked out that I didn't even want any seconds of roast potatoes, and they are my absolute faves.

Me and Tilda helped with the drying up and I was a bit quiet but hopefully she didn't notice. When we went back up and carried on with the cushions I didn't mention anything about my thinkings, but there was this weird feeling between us as if she was having some thinkings of her own but wasn't saying anything either.

It was fine, though, and we still had loads of

fun, but now I am completely in confusion about what thinkings to think. I'm still a bit worried that the Veruschka person won't notice Dad's 5 key bad-points. (I wish I knew where she lived so I could send her a list of them.) Also, what if Mum gets a date too – with Mr. Van der Zwan! Mum can't *possibly* fancy him, can she? I mean, it is *Mr. Van der Zwan*! But what if she does and they get married and he becomes my stepfather and he is as stricty with me as he is with Tilda? Argh! That would be a total nightmare!

Oh, all these confusing thoughts are whirling and twirling through my brain now, like about Dad marrying a wicked stepmother and having more children with her and ignoring me and Alex, and Mum marrying Mr. VDZ and me having to wear a cagoule and embarrassing sandals and go to bed at 9 p.m. *every* night and not drink Coke or watch *Vice Squad*, like, ever.

Whaaaaaa! I feel like my brain is melting.

Mon 24th

Half-term – yippeeee!!!
I'm writing this while gulping
down some cereal mega-quickly 'cos
Mum won't let me go round Tilda's
without eating something first.

Tilda has just called me to tell me something so
totally and utterly *amazing* I don't know if you
will even believe me! Well, she picked up her
e-mails (that should give you a clue about what
the *amazing* thing is) and…

Yes…

WE HAVE BEEN CHOSEN TO
GO ON THE TV SHOW!!!

How totally fab is that?! She had to hang on
while I ran round the house jumping up and down
and going, "Yeeeeeeeeessssssssssssss!!!!!!" and I could

hear her yelling, "Lucy, come back!" down the phone!!!

And – even fabber – it is going to be on Friday because this group of boys have dropped out 'cos of having flu! *Yeeeeeesss*!!! (I mean, not *Yeeeeeesss*!!! that they have flu, obviously, but *Yeeeeeesss*!!! that we can be on TV instead of them!)

Mum says she can come up to London with us on Friday – how cool is that? Tilda e-mailed them my number 'cos of it being my mum who is taking us, and a researcher (which is this person who organizes stuff for the show) called Jaime rang up and went through all the arrangements with Mum while I hovered excitedly around trying to listen in.

When I finally got to speak to Jaime, she asked if we've got a camcorder to film the room makeover 'cos they have got this idea to do a before and after thing using the pix that Tilda already sent them. I said yes 'cos Dad has one and so that is sort of like us having one. Then she was like, "See you on Friday — we're so excited about meeting you!" and I went, "Us too! We are mega-ly excited about meeting you and going on telly! Will it actually be **ON** on Friday?"

Jaime explained that it wouldn't, 'cos it isn't live, but how it will be on in a few months' time and how they'll definitely let us know when. When I got off the phone I spent about 3½ more minutes just running round the house and leaping up and down going, "*Yeeeeeeeeeeessssss!!!!!!*" with excitement about going on the show.

Then after I had taken a few deep breaths I rang Dad and told him about the fab news and he said fine about borrowing the camcorder and how he reckoned we could finish the room in time if we worked really hard. Then he said how about if we did a shot with him driving us up to Tilda's in his new car then leaping out with his tool belt on and introducing himself as "Brian Hartley, DIY action hero!"

I was thinking *Noooooooo!!!!* but I said,

"Yeah, maybe," 'cos he has been so cool about helping us I don't want to completely spoil all his fun. I didn't say anything about *The Dreaded Date* and neither did he — hopefully it went wrong for all the reasons I mentioned before.

Then I got showered and dressed and put some eyeshadow on and did my hair in a cool style to keep it out of the way of purple paint, all in a flash of lightning (i.e. v. fast, with spending only about 17 mins in the bathroom!).

Now I have finished my cereal Mum is dropping me round at Tilda's so gotta go! It was hard holding the spoon in my left hand while writing this and quite a lot of milk did dribble down my chin but at least I have told you the exciting news! **BTW** I had an extra half a bowl to finish off the packet so I can recycle the cardboard. So I am v. v. full now (groan!) but that is the cost of being a *Goddess of Green*!

We have just finished lunch round Tilda's

and I am writing this in her upstairs bathroom 'cos I wanted to update you on how everything is going!

$\mathcal{U}$s three are mega-ly excited about going on the TV show, and we kept non-stop talking about what we think it will be like and about whether afterwards we will be famous and get recognized in the street and asked for our autographs. Mine is like this:

Lucy Jessica Hartley X.

But I might have to come up with a new one specially. I also need to decide on which new smile I am definitely having so that I can do it on the TV show. We are working massively hard to get everything done by the end of Thursday but we are so excited that we don't even feel tired at all!

Here is the official update on our green project progress:

1. Dad came round just after me and Jules got here and we finished painting all the walls.
2. He started glossing the skirting boards and the wooden bits round the doors with this cool eco-gloss paint that doesn't smell as bad as the normal stuff.
3. Me, Jules and Tilda started painting the chest of drawers and the wardrobe. We meant to do them on Saturday but I have found out that when you are doing a room makeover everything takes longer than you think.

Oh, and guess what! When it was time to clear out the chest of drawers and the wardrobe before painting them, Tilda went all red and flustery and she kept trying to give us two other jobs to do, like getting some fizzy water from the fridge, or a sponge from the bathroom, or some kitchen roll from the, er, kitchen (duh, obviously!). When we came back we found her trying to quickly stuff some things into plastic bags without us seeing and I realized that's why she was trying to get us out of the room! She didn't want us to see what they were, but her cringitis fate was sealed 'cos just then Mr. VDZ came out of his study with a big load of papers and he stopped in and picked something out of one of the bags.

Well. It was a pair of the most hideous trousers I have ever seen in my whole actual 13 years and (erm, hang on while I work it out) 67 days of being alive on this planet of Earth. Seriously, my eyes were popping out in **GOBSMACKED FLABBERGASTATION**. Tilda obviously thought so too 'cos she was trying to block our view of them. But Mr. VDZ held up the hideous trousers and said, "Matilda-Jane, you haven't worn these lovely slacks for yonks."

I was thinking, *What are slacks?* and also, *What are yonks?*

Tilda went absolutely burning red, say like a 9½ on the *Cringe-o-meter* scale.

Then he took more things out of the bag, like yucky tops and horrible skirts that were like the actual correct school ones Mr. Cain tries to make us wear but in all different colours. Who would wear a skirt like that out of choice when not actually at school? Maybe Tilda used to, but she was obviously wishing they had all just *spontaneously combusted* (which is when things suddenly burst into flames for no reason), 'cos now she has cool stuff in her hippyish style that really suits her.

Mr. VDZ was saying, "Things do get forgotten at the back of the wardrobe, don't they? It's so good you've rediscovered them."

Then he pulled out the most revolting item I have ever seen in my entire life.

He was like, "I love this pullover. It will be nice

to see you wearing it
again." It was the
kind of jumper that
could make you
vomit on the spot,
even if you hadn't
eaten any off curry

or anything, but just by
looking at it. Tilda did a little laugh and said,
"Well, maybe, I'll have to see if it still fits."

Jules was about to say something and I had to
give her a quick kick on the ankle to remind her
that Tilda was only saying that to save her dad's
feelings and had not gone suddenly insane.

When Mr. VDZ went back into his study
again, Tilda was just standing there frozen to the
spot with total fashion embarrassment. Me and
Jules were staring at her in utter horrification and
Jules did finally say, "You're not actually going
to *wear* those things, are you?"

Tilda shuddered and hissed, "No, I'm not! I

82

just didn't want to hurt Dad's feelings!" Then she sighed and added, "I don't like the thought of wasting them, though. It's a shame to just throw them away, and not very environmental. Maybe I could give them to a charity shop."

But just then I was struck by a second big Creative Inspiration!

I dipped into the bag and pulled out a green skirt which was in fact not too bad, and a long cardigan and a silky purple shirt thing that would have been nice if it didn't have this vile lacy collar.

Urgh!

Double urgh!

Triple urgh!

My *Creative Inspiration* had totally taken me over by then and I tipped out the bag and was rummaging through, holding things up against me and trying them next to each other and going, "If you cut here, and take a piece of material from here and add some funky necklaces to this and…"

Tilda stared at me. "Lucy, are you saying that—" she began.

"Yes, we can recycle your old clothes to create fab new outfits! Then we can wear them on TV on Friday!"

"Not that horse-head jumper, though, surely?" said Jules, looking horrified, and then she was like, "Lucy, even though you are a fashion genius, that is just never going to look good whatever we do to it." (BTW, I would not normally write that I am a fashion genius, 'cos it would sound like I have a massivo head, but that is what she did honestly say.)

"Okay," I said agreeingly. "It's just too horrible – I mean, special."

I quickly changed it to that in case Tilda was upset but she didn't seem bothered

Then I went back to rummaging through the bags, saying things like, "If you altered this skirt hem or put a belt on this top..." and Tilda was getting all excited but Jules still looked like she wanted to throw the clothes off the edge of a very high cliff. I could see she was not exactly getting just how fab my recycled fashion idea was – so I quickly thought of a way to persuade her.

I pulled out a shapeless black top and held it up. "If we cut the sleeves off this and give it a jagged neckline and pull out the side seam and put it back together with safety pins it'll make such a cool top for you!"

Jules *still* didn't look convinced so I grabbed an old envelope off Tilda's desk and did a quick sketch of my idea for the top in a swish-swish fashion-designer-ish way. Oh, hang on, it's in my bag. I'll just stick it in here.

Jules started getting keen too, then (*finally!*).
She said thanks and how she thought the recycled
clothes project was a great idea and also when
would the top be ready?

HA-HA-HAAAAAA!

Evil-genius laugh!

See, I knew I could persuade her!

Oh, hang on, Jules and Tilda are ready to start
painting again and they are asking where I am.

Bye!!

I have nipped into Tilda's downstairs loo

Argh! My ears! My ears! I think they are going to fall off with the shock!

Dad's phone just rang while we were painting the wardrobe and instead of answering it with us there, he went outside to talk. I just happened to go downstairs to get a drink of water at that same moment and I just popped out the kitchen door for some fresh air and I just had a little stroll round to the front of the house to stretch my legs and I just stood behind this nice green bush admiring its speckledy leaves and by total coincidence I just accidentally happened to hear what Dad was saying.

Yes, you've guessed it – he was talking to the Veruschka person. I can't bear to write down his exact words in here (if I do my brain might explode with mortification) so I will just tell you that he was saying revolting slushy stuff like boy bands sing about. And then he said he would phone her later to arrange meeting up again.

So the date didn't go wrong after all!

ARGH and DOUBLE ARGH!

At home

Guess what? Tilda has had a FABULASTIC idea!

I am lying on my bed, writing this and texting with Jules and Tilda and listening to my new Jess Moon album all at the same time.

When Dad came back upstairs at Tilda's I had to act like I hadn't just heard anything *hideous*. Dad smiled at me and I did a pretend smile back but I couldn't find one bit of real smiliness in me. I really wanted to ask him what was going on but I just couldn't make any words come out. But also, I sort of didn't want to know in case it was really serious between them, in a wicked-stepmother-type way.

Argh!

So now I don't know what to think.

Okay. Deep breath.

Huuuuuuuuuuuuuuuuuuuuuuuuur!

That is me taking the deep breath, BTW

I am going to push it out of my mind by thinking about something else.

WE'RE GOING ON TELLY!!! WE'RE GOING ON TELLY!!! WE'RE GOING ON TELLY!!! WE'RE GOING ON TELLY!!! WE'RE GOING ON TELLY!!!

That's better.

So anyway, we finished doing the wardrobe and the chest of drawers – they ended up looking really cool and hippyish like this:

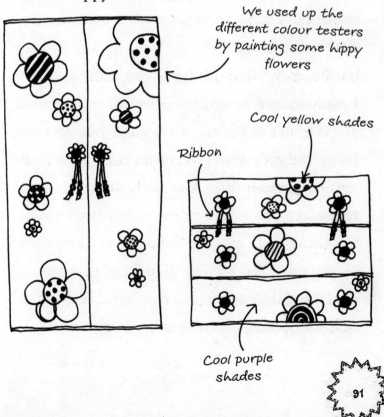

We used up the different colour testers by painting some hippy flowers

Ribbon

Cool yellow shades

Cool purple shades

Dad finished the gloss and the room looks really amazing already, even though everything isn't back in its place. We all said a big thanks to him and even Tilda and Jules gave him a hug, and I got this feeling of how lovely he is, even with all his embarrassingness. Mr. VDZ came to say thanks too and Dad swaggered his tool belt about a bit and said, "No probs, dude," which means *You're welcome* in normal language. Then he had to go to the radio station and get ready for his show tonight.

The very-nearly-finished-ness of the almost-made-over-room must have given Tilda an idea 'cos she suddenly burst out saying, "I know, we could have a sleepover to celebrate my new room!"

I thought Mr. VDZ was going to say *No way, José!* 'cos he is *that* stricty, but in fact he said, "That's a good idea. You can put everything back in tomorrow and then do all the finishing touches and have a sleepover tomorrow night, if it's okay with your parents, of course."

When Mum came to get us she said yes, and these are the texts I have been just getting (and sending!) while writing this:

Jules: I cn slpovr too. Cool beans!

Tilda: That is brilliant!

Me: Fabulissimo!

Jules: Shall I bring some Wotsits and Coke?

We had to wait a really long time to get the reply from Tilda 'cos she likes to write things out in proper language, but when it got here it said:

Okay, cool, but don't show my dad 'cos he might say we can only have cereal bars and OJ for our midnight feast. If that happens, don't worry 'cos we can all pile into the bottom of the wardrobe and have the Wotsits and Coke in secret!

That sounded like so much fun, even better than just being allowed to have Wotsits and Coke in the first place!

When we were still at Tilda's waiting to get picked up, she said, "There is one thing we have to sort out, though, before we have a cool sleepover," and then she reached under her pillow and pulled out this revolting nightie like

When we had all stopped giggling, she explained how her dad bought it for her ages ago and she just sort of carried on wearing it without noticing how embarrassing it was, but now she wants a fab and groovy new look for the sleepover. So when we go to town to get the crisps and stuff for tomorrow night we'll head to New Look as well and see what we can find to turn Tilda into a groovacious sleepover babe!

All the room stuff is done now except for putting everything back and also there is still the question of what to put on the walls for pictures. The recycled rug even got delivered yesterday, after Mr. VDZ had ordered it on the net for us from that website I found (with hardly *any* help from Simon Driscott!).

Also we have drawn more hippy flowers on the yellow wall and used leftover purple paint to colour them in and they look *sooooo* cool.

That gave us the idea to do frames on the purple walls but painted actually *on* the wall in the yellow paint, like this:

It looks really funky but we haven't got any posters to go in them yet. Tilda's into maths but there aren't exactly posters of that, are there? She also does kind of like a few pop stars but she's not *that* keen on them. I have ripped out some pages from mags with cool ads and fashion features on and they will have to do for the meantime until we think of something better.

I have brought the stuff for our recycled outfits home so I can come up with the final designs, and I'm going to get on with that 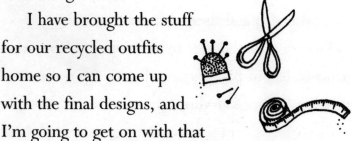 now. (Also, Tilda said she's going to quickly e-mail the *Go Green!* people to let them know about our fab outfit idea!)

Bye!

PS Oh, this green project is turning out to be *soooooo* cool!

Tuesday 25th

Sleepover Day - yippeeeeeeee!!!!

We met in town this morning (me and Jules walked there which Mum says is fine as long as we stay together) and Tilda drove there (you know what I mean, i.e. her dad drove her there, not that she has suddenly become 17 by magic!). I gave Mr. VDZ my half-done *Go Green!* show outfits to take back with him 'cos I am going to fit them on Jules and Tilda at the sleepover and maybe they can even help me with some of the sewing.

Oh yeah, and we got the stuff for our midnight feast. We are making fairy cakes and we bought all these cool things to go on the top from this little baking shop in town, like silver balls and bluebells made out of icing that has gone hard in a jar, and sprinkles and everything.

We also went to New Look to get a cool New Look for Tilda (how spooky that the shop is actually called that!) for the sleepover. Even though we are the Queens of Green, we still do need to buy *some* new things, 'cos there's no way I could have recycled that old nightie into funkiness! Her New Look is like this:

The eye-masky thing was so cool that me and Jules got one each as well, so we will all be asleep like:

Jules and Tilda are saying to me *hurry up, stop writing in there* 'cos they want to put everything back in Tilda's room and do the finishing touches and then get ready for the sleepover.

YIPPPEEEEE!!!!

I am so massively excited I can hardly wait!

Well, it is just before the
actual proper sleepovery
bit of the sleepover
and I wanted to quickly tell
you something...

When Mum picked us up from town and dropped
us off here, she stayed for a cup of tea and
a big laughy chat with Mr. VDZ for about half an
hour (making me even more certain that they have
feelings of likingness for each other – *bleugh*!). I
didn't have to see them luckily, 'cos me, Jules and
Tilda slipped off upstairs to put up the sari-
curtains Mum's friend Gloria donated to us. BTW,
she also let us have her recycled bottle lamp 'cos
she reckons she can get another one quite easily.
What a star!

The finished room looked completely fab and
Tilda was in GOBSMACKED FLABBERGASTATION
about its grooviness. I will draw it all properly to

show you soon, but not right now 'cos my **BFF** are calling me downstairs to help ice the fairy cakes. We made them earlier and now they have cooled we're going to do loads of different designs with the sprinkles etc. and make them look totally gorge.

I have woken up first!

Only 2 days till we go on TV – yippeeeeee!!!

Even though it is 8.47 a.m. Jules and Tilda are still asleep. Mr. VDZ is being nice and not making us get up early to have a cold shower or go for a 5k run or whatever stricty dads make you do. If I'm really quiet I can write in here without waking my **BFF** up, and tell you all the cool and most secretly secret stuff that happened at the sleepover.

I just have to draw you a pic of the fairy cakes because they came out really lovely:

One of those icing bluebells I mentioned about →

White icing

Sugarified rose petals

Multicoloured sprinkles on powder-blue icing

silver balls on candy pink icing

Lilac icing

Plus, they were delish too — I know 'cos we had some after tea (which Tilda called supper and which of course was very healthy  and involved many different vegetables,  but we didn't mind too much 'cos we knew we were having a cool midnight feast later on!).

Before we properly started the sleepover, we sorted out the recycled outfits for the *Go Green!* show. I showed Jules and Tilda my designs and luckily they totally loved them (phew!). After loads of trying on and taking off and swapping round and pinning up and adding buttons and sewing and more trying on and taking off and me having a couple of last-minute different ideas and more sewing and then some experimenting with accessories, we had our final recycled outfits.

Oh, hang on, I drew pix of us to stick in here but I have got no glue. I'll just get Tilda's Pritt Stick to put them in.

♥ JULES ♥

♥ TILDA ♥

BTW, Jules and Tilda were posing for me when I was drawing them in their recycled outfits so it was a bit like drawing a still life although they did not keep still at all, especially Jules, who kept fidgeting, so it was more like a moving life. Tilda drew the pic of me – good, isn't it?

Oh, whoops, I tripped over when I got the Pritt Stick and knocked a pencil pot off Tilda's desk and now they are waking up. So, gotta go, but I'll carry on writing in here as soon as poss!

Still Wednesday,

but now it is 12.41 precisely.

I am back at home now, and I have just woken up. I had a little lie-down 'cos of being so tired from staying up whispering most of last night! At the actual sleepover itself loads of things happened. Oh, hey, I know – because sleepovers are top secret I am going to write all the things that we did in a top secret code and you can work out what they were.

enituor ecnad a pu edam ew

pu, edam – ew!

pwoepactoern

psychically other tried each to
send to messages we

Do you have
a crush on
anyone?

Shall we
get matching
ballet flats for
school?

We had a...

Mmm, yummy!

This is our list of how okay
the okay boys in our class are

Jamie Cousins	78%
Bill Cripps	84%
Ben Jones	75%
Charlie P	71%
Simon Driscott	34%

I put him in 'cos even though he is quite geeky,
SD is quite funny and plus he did help me with
the web surfing for our room makeover

108

We also excitedly imagined being on TV and practised saying things about the room makeover and our recycled outfits in our televisiony voices. BTW, I so cannot believe we are going on *Go Green!* Hang on while I just pinch myself to make sure it is not a dream.

OW!!!

It is in fact definitely real (and now I have got the bruise to prove it). How **AWESOME**, as some Americans would say. I might start saying that too 'cos I like things that are American in general.

While practising for being on TV, we all got the hysterical giggles (or *the sillies*, as Mum calls it) and our sides were nearly splitting, even though that is only a saying and not a real thing that can happen. We were rolling round on the cool new eco-rug in these total hysterics when Mr. VDZ walked in and said, "All right, girls, I don't want to be a killjoy but I think it's time you settled down now," and even though it was only just past 10 p.m. we said yes okay, 'cos that is one hour

later than Tilda's normal bedtime so we knew that
Mr. VDZ was actually being quite nice to us
considering how stricty he normally is. So we all
did a good impression of looking like butter
wouldn't melt in our mouths, like this:

Not melting!

When actually we were secretly planning to
have more fun instead of going to sleep, like this:

Evil genius
grin!

So we got into bed, with Tilda in her bed and me and Jules sharing a cool blow-up mattress thing on the floor next to her. It creaked every time we moved, like a door in a haunted house, making us giggle. We got *the sillies* again and we had to stuff our hands in our mouths so Mr. VDZ would not hear, and then when we'd calmed down we had a big whisper about how Freya Smith is so obviously trying to take Keisha away from Jackie and Bella in PE even though those three have been **BFF** for as long as me and Jules can remember.

Then we had our midnight feast. It was only 11.23 p.m. but we couldn't wait any longer!

Afterwards we settled down a bit and we were talking about secret girl stuff like Qs (**BTW**, Q is our code for *period*, so we don't have to loudly say **PERIOD** in public when boys are listening, but now we just say Q *all* the time anyway). Jules recently got hers so now it is only me who hasn't (boo!). Hopefully it will hurry up and come soon! Anyway, 'cos we were talking quietly about serious stuff I started thinking about Dad and that Veruschka person again and I ended up mentioning it to Tilda and Jules (of course I didn't say anything about my secret suspicions about Mum and Mr. VDZ – Tilda would go mad if I even just *slightly* suggested that).

Tilda's idea was to just talk to Dad and tell him about my worries. It was nice of her to suggest it, but I was like, *Yeah right!* I would be **WAY** too embarrassed to talk to Dad like that! Jules's idea was to find out where Dad and Veruschka are going next and then make the date go wrong somehow. I went, "Good thinking," but then we couldn't work out any ways to wreck it, even if we could find out where it was, so I couldn't do that idea either.

Then I had a **REVELATION** that was so sudden it made me sit bolt upright with amazedness. "I know what I have to do," I told Tilda and Jules. "I have to get Mum and Dad back together."

Jules and Tilda were going "What???" and you are most probably going "What???" too, but let me just explain my thinking and then you will totally get where I am coming from.

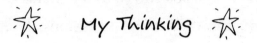 My Thinking

1. Things are only okay now between Mum and Dad 'cos they are not seeing anyone else, i.e. so there are no stricty stepfathers or wicked stepmothers to ruin it.
2. The only way to make sure they don't get together with anyone else is to make them get back together with each other.
3. So, you can see it is actually most scientifically logical that they should.
4. But when I said it to Jules and Tilda I didn't mention stricty stepfathers, of course!

Tilda went, "Lucy, that's crazy!"
But I was like, "No, it's genius!"
Tilda did a big groan of despair and went, "It's almost one o'clock. I'm going to sleep. Goodnight!"

But luckily Jules did get the geniusness of my idea, so we carried on whispering and came up with a fab plan, which I wrote down while she shone her torchlight on my paper.

The Parent Plan

1. I tell Mum that Gloria (her friend) rang and invited her for a girly night out at TGI Fridays at the retail park.
2. I say Gloria is picking her up at 7.30 p.m.
3. In actuality, Gloria doesn't know anything about it.
4. I arrange for Dad to look after us.
5. Dad comes round.
6. When Gloria doesn't come, I suddenly "remember" that she rang to cancel.
7. I say, "Seeing as Dad is already here now he may as well have tea with us."
8. I make Alex come upstairs with me while Mum and Dad have tea together and chat and get on even better than they are doing already.
9. They realize they still love each other.
10. Et voila, they get back together.

So that means no wicked stepmother for me!

HA-HA-HAAAAAAAAAAAA!!!!

Evil-genius laugh!

Oh, hang on a sec… Mum wants something –
she keeps calling "Lucy!" up the stairs and I keep
going, "What?" but she still isn't coming up so I
suppose I'll have to go and see what it is. Argh!
If only she knew I was up here planning how to
sort her life out for her, she wouldn't be
distracting me!

Still Wednesday,

but now it's 2.02 p.m.
Mum only wanted me to have
a sandwich, then bring my sleepover
stuff upstairs and sort it out.

Which reminds me, just to quickly finish off
telling you about the sleepover, when Jules and
Tilda woke up this morning we were all really
hungry 'cos it was later than we usually have
breakfast. We took the rest of the fairy cakes
downstairs and Jules pretended to be a waitress
and me and Tilda ordered silly combinations of
things and she had to come up with them, like
Coco Pops on toast and fairy cakes dipped in milk.
It was so funny and luckily it was ages before Mr.
VDZ came in and told us to be sensible. After that
we just had to eat things normally, like cornflakes
with milk, and toast with jam – *yawn*.

Then we filmed Tilda's room with Dad's

116

camcorder and now I have time to show you all the stuff we did and the end result and how fab it all looked.

We panned the camera round the room in one go and took everything in, and then we went back and did pix of each little bit. Jules wanted to be in every shot sort of going "Ta-daa!" next to things with her arms out, but I said it was probably better to just focus on the objects. She nearly got in a *dark and stormy* mood with me then so I did

let her wear the feather boa and give a
demonstration of the mirror.

When Jules's mum came to get us, we said
thanks to Mr. VDZ and Jules said what a cool dad
he is for letting us have the sleepover and you
could tell he was really happy about that. Then
Jules whispered "*Good luck*" to me for the Parent
Plan and Tilda gave me a look to mean *You are a*

crazy person *and it will never work*, but I just did my *mysterious* smile at her (which I have now decided is my fave one, **BTW**).

I have got the camcorder footage of the room ready to go and I keep imagining what I'm going to say on TV over and over again, and I'm so excited about going on the show I might actually **EXPLODE**. Like, just now I was trying to watch *Friends* on E4 but instead I just found myself staring at the actual television itself, as in at the plastic bit, thinking, *We're going to be ON there!*

Now I'm going to try and calmly and quietly get on with my final checks on our

recycled outfits for going on TV!!!

I said I'd add more safety pins to Jules's top because the side was gaping open a bit, and I'm also going to finish putting the final sequins on Tilda's skirt.

As part of my cunning Parent Plan I have offered to cook for me, Dad and Alex tonight (and Mum, secretly, but at the mo she has believed me about Gloria inviting her out and is right now doing her nails in Paint The Town Red!). My speciality is lasagne but we have run out of packets of the white sauce stuff you need for it, so it'll have to be tuna pasta bake instead. Fingers crossed that will still work!

Still, still, still
Wednesday
8.25 p.m. ce soir.

Well, I can report that the Parent Plan is going fab-ly so far. I encouraged Mum to wear her lovely red dress, and she did, even though she was going, "Lucy, it's only TGI Fridays, not The Ritz."

I got on with the tea and when she came downstairs she looked *amazing*. Dad came round while I was setting the table and I nearly gave the game away by doing four places, but I remembered at the last minute to do three because Mum was supposed to be going out. When Dad saw Mum his eyes popped almost entirely out of his head and he said how nice she looked, and I was thinking, *Ha! Take THAT, Veruschka person!*

Mum and Dad were chatting while I was tossing the salad and trying to be invisible (difficult for me!) and in the end Mum noticed it was

121

getting later and later and Gloria still hadn't come so she said, "I'll just give her a ring," and that's when I did my fake pretending to remember thing and went,

Oh no! I'm so sorry, I forgot to say that Gloria rang when you went to the corner shop earlier and she said she was ill and how she can't come. It completely slipped out of my mind.

Mum stared at me and she was like, "What?" and asking how I could have let her get ready and everything, and going on about my brain being like a sieve. I really wanted to say, No it is not, but of course I had to stand there and put up with being told off for the good of the Parent Plan. Then Mum said something I didn't expect which was,

"Well, Gloria must be very ill to not want to go out. I'd better call and see if she needs anything." She reached for the phone and I went, "No!" really loudly and I had to think of an excuse on the spot. Luckily I had a *Creative Inspiration* to go, "I've just this second remembered that she said she has a migraine and she's got the right tablets already so you don't need to go round and take her anything, and she's just going to go to bed and fall asleep so there's no need to ring her up or you will in fact be disturbing her and making her feel worse."

Mum and Dad were both staring at me in this way like they were only just on the edge of believing what I was saying, so I quickly changed the subject and went, "Now you're here, Dad, you can stay and have some supper with us 'cos by a lucky chance there is loads." And I quickly set the other place at the table and called Alex down from playing his Playstation. Of course, Mum will eventually find out the truth from Gloria but by then, fingers crossed, she will be back together with Dad and she will be too busy thanking me to be annoyed!

I set some candles from the living room on the table for romantic purposes and lit them with the cooks' matches out of the drawer. Mum looked confusedly at them and went, "Are we expecting a power cut?"

"No, I'm saving electricity to help the planet," I said, doing some more quick thinking.

Mum was still quite bewildered, luckily, so she left the candles burning and we all sat down and I kept chatting all the time so she couldn't think about the weirdness of what had happened with Gloria. When Alex finished his tuna pasta bake he started telling Dad about what they did at Junior Karate this week, but I interruptingly went, "Alex, I have just noticed that it is quite late and nearly your bedtime." Mum realized too then and said she'd take him upstairs (you have to actually WATCH him brush his teeth or he simply does not

124

do it) but I went, "No, you stay here and relax, I'll go." Mum and Dad were having wine so I topped up their glasses, then grabbed Alex and bundled him out of the kitchen. He was really cross with me for making Mum remember his bedtime, but he will thank me in the future when Mum and Dad are back together and we are safe from wicked stepmothers and stricty stepfathers. As I dragged Alex upstairs, I heard Dad say to Mum, "Is she always this helpful?"

Mum laughed and went, "I wish!"

Charming, n'est-ce pas?

Instead of going back down again I have stayed upstairs and it has been over one hour now and Dad is still here. Hang on, I am just going to creep down and listen at the door...

2 mins later

Yessity-yes-yes!!!

They are talking and laughing and Dad just said he will open another bottle of wine. It's working – my plan is working!

HA-HA-HAAAAAA!!!

↑

Evil-genius laugh again!

I'll pop down really quickly and say goodnight so Mum doesn't get distracted from Dad by coming to check I've gone to bed.

Thursday at 8.23 a.m.

We're going on TV TOMORROW!!!

I am trying to eat my cornflakes in the mess that is all over the table — can you believe that Mum and Dad haven't even put the pasta dish in the sink to soak or cleared up the wine bottles?! That is really unusual for Mum because normally she insists on doing the washing-up straight away after we've eaten (and we have to do the drying). In fact, she is not even **UP** yet and Alex is watching TV in his pyjamas.

I will clear up the mess and get Alex some cereal. Yuck — there are little bits of dried tuna stuck onto the plates! Still, it will be worth a bit of cleaning when M and D are back together! It should only take a few more times of them hanging out to do the trick, and then Dad won't be interested in the Veruschka person any more and Mum won't be keen on Mr. VDZ. Hee hee!!

<u>10.43 a.m.</u>
Oh dear. I am sorry to
tell you that I have just
been having a massive cry!

I am okay now, though, so don't worry. What
happened was, I'd just done all the clearing up and
given Alex some cereal, then sent him upstairs to
get dressed when Mum came down in her bath
robe and started going through the box of
medicine she keeps on top of the cupboards,
looking for headache tablets.

My happy mood 'cos of the Parent Plan success
was still going then, so I got her to sit down at the
kitchen table and made her a cup of tea. I was just
about to go upstairs and leave her to think about
how nice Dad in fact is, when she said, "Hang on a
minute, Lucy, I think we need to have a little chat."

I was thinking, *Wow, that was fast! She
is going to tell me they're getting back*

together already! But in actual fact she was not going to say that.

Instead she said, "I'm going to call Gloria now and see how she is."

I went, "Um, okay, but I have just remembered she did say that the tablets take, like, two days to work and she won't be able to talk on the phone 'cos—"

But Mum cut me off, going, "Lucy, Gloria never did arrange to go out with me last night, did she? And she's not ill at all, is she?"

I was going to say *yes* and *yes* to that, but I somehow knew that she knew what I was up to and that there was no point, so I just shook my head.

Mum sighed and took my hand. "Lucy, sweetheart, I thought you understood that your dad and I aren't ever going to get back together—" she began.

"I did!" I exclaimed interruptingly (or interrupted exclaimingly). "But this is an emergency." I really didn't want to say the next thing, 'cos I thought it might make her upset, but she had to understand. I took a deep breath and garbled out, "He had a date with this woman called Veruschka who most probably wears a Tiny Denim Miniskirt and has razor-sharp nails and kicks puppies, and he's seeing her again!"

I thought Mum would dissolve into tears then, but she just sort of half smiled and said, "I know, we talked about it last night."

I was shocked that she didn't seem to mind, but then *someone* dissolved into tears, and that someone was me. "But what if he marries her and she's a wicked stepmother and takes him away from me and Alex?" I blurted out, between sobbing.

Mum pulled me onto her lap and even though I am a very actual teenager now, I let her. "It's not just Dad," I splurgled, with all my emotionality coming out at once. "What about you and Mr. Van der Zwan?"

Mum almost spat her tea out all over me then. "What?" she spluttered. "Lucy, there's nothing going on between me and Christiaan!"

"*Really* not?" I asked, sniffling and gulping in a v. v. unattractive way.

"No!" she cried. "Really, *really* not. We're just friends."

I was *massively* relieved about that.

"Good," I said, "and if you could just promise never to go out with anyone ever until I am mega-ly old like about 23 that would be excellent. Thanks."

Mum sighed. "I can't promise that, love," she said. "It's not easy being a single parent, you know."

"But I thought it was okay 'cos you've got me to help with Alex and now you have *Grabbed Life With Both Hands* by doing the make-up course you'll soon have the job of your dreams and be going round the world doing Kate Moss for Burberry, and you won't have time to even think about getting a boyfriend, will you?" I asked, hoping not. "I mean, you don't want one, do you?" I added, even more hoping not.

Mum smiled then and squeezed my hand. "No, I'm fine without one at the moment, Lu," she said, sort of half laughing. "It might be nice to meet someone in time, but right now I'm just interested in people as friends."

That made me feel better, as even though Mum had not in fact promised to *never* meet anyone else (my *ideal* situation), she is obviously not about to suddenly get a boyfriend next week or anything, and definitely not Mr. VDZ.

Mum squeezed my shoulders and I cried a bit more 'cos for some reason I couldn't seem to help it, but then gradually I stopped sniffling and gulping and calmed down.

"If it's any consolation, Dad saw Veruschka again yesterday and it didn't quite work out," Mum said then.

I stared blinkingly at her, going, "But why?"

She sighed. "Oh, you know. They just didn't

really click in the end. It's not that easy to find someone you really hit it off with." Then she added, "And I guess the fact that *that* car broke down on the back road to Purse Caundle and they had to wait over an hour in that cold wind for Uncle Ken to rescue them didn't help." We both couldn't help giggling a bit then, even though we were trying not to.

"It's a shame it didn't work out for him, though," Mum said after we had calmed down.

"No, it's not!" I exclaimed. "He shouldn't *want* to have a girlfriend anyway. I wish things could just stay the same as they are now."

Mum moved me onto another chair, 'cos I was getting heavy, and then she said, "You can't stop things changing, Lu. But don't worry, neither your dad or I are going to rush into anything, and I've made him promise that if he does meet someone else he won't keep it from you in future. We'll make sure you and Alex have the chance to talk about your feelings."

"Good," I said. And I do feel better now. Maybe, looking back at it, the thing that most freaked me out was the idea of everything just changing really suddenly and me having no choice about it. I'm so glad Mum has promised that won't happen.

I still feel a bit teary and trembly, though, so I am taking some *Deep Cleansing Breaths*, as Mum calls them.

I'm just going to check how red and puffy my face still looks in the bathroom mirror, then lay out all the recycled outfits for our **TV APPEARANCE** tomorrow (!!!) on my bed, 'cos Mum is coming up to see them all finished. She's doing our make-up for the show so she's going to decide what look will go with each outfit. How fab – while we're talking about it I think I'll secretly pretend that I am a *Real Actual Fashion Designer* discussing her latest collection with the make-up artist before her catwalk show! That will definitely cheer me up!

134

9.07 p.m.

Me and Jules and Tilda rang each other about 25 times today to check the plans for tomorrow and say final things to each other and just generally go *eeeeeekkkkkkkkk!!!* together about going on TV!

BTW, Mum loved the recycled designs and she even said I can wear my special-occasion high heels with my outfit (I am not allowed to wear them very often 'cos she has this thing about how my feet will grow all weird and twisted if I do). Right, I am going to bed now to get some beauty sleep so I look good for tomorrow.

Goodnight!

Later

I have tried to read in bed but I am too excited!!!

11.37 p.m.

I am supposed to be asleep getting my beauty zzzs so I look okay and not hideous on TV tomorrow, but I am still too *skipping through the tulips* and I can't even concentrate on sleeping!

That is my phrase that I made up to mean over the moon, BTW, so I don't have to keep saying over the moon all the time!

12.02 a.m.

Urgh! Still too excited to sleep even though I am massively, massively tired. I hope I can sleep soon or all you will see on TV are my giant eye bags! Yuck! I know, I will try counting sheep leaping over a fence. No, that is boring. Instead, I'll count models walking down a catwalk!

12.23 a.m.

I will have to stop counting models now. I have counted 876 so far and I am sti

FRIDAY!!!!

THE DAY IS FINALLY HERE!!!
WE ARE RIGHT NOW ON THE
TRAIN GOING TO THE TV STUDIO!!!!

Well, the train has finally stopped doing this bumpy uppy-and-downy thing, so I can write in here. We are *soooooo* mega-ly excited to be on our way to London. We are all sitting in a four-seat bit with a table and, amazingly, Mum let us get some drinks and biscuits from the buffet. Usually she says how *extortionate* they are and brings something from home!

Tilda just helped me spell that, BTW!

I am sitting by the window next to Mum going forwards, opposite Jules who is next to Tilda and who is going backwards (duh, obviously!). We have all got our own handbags and we are keeping our tickets in them instead of Mum looking after them

138

for all of us, which would be CRINGE-TASTICALLY babyish.

We're not wearing our fab outfits yet 'cos Mum thought we might crease them up or spill juice on them or something (v. v. likely, knowing me!). Instead we are wearing our normal clothes and normal tiny bit of make-up, which for me = some purple eyeliner, smoky grey shadow, a weeny slick of mascara and my fave Very Berry Glide-On Liptint, and for Jules = quite a lot of black eyeliner and mascara, and for Tilda = nothing apart from some cherry lipsalve.

BTW, when Mum was buying the tickets, I huddled me and Jules and Tilda together on the platform and told them about what happened with the Parent Plan and also about the chat I had with Mum. I accidentally let it slip out that I had been worried not just about Dad but also about Mum and Mr. VDZ. Tilda looked outraged so I quickly said, "No, it's okay, don't worry, she doesn't fancy him." But then she got all huffity going, "Well, what's *wrong* with him?" and then we all burst into laughing because I couldn't win whatever I said. In a serious way under the laughing I kind of know Tilda half thought the same as me and that she is also relieved that Mum and her dad are only sort of friends with no fancying going on whatsoever (in fact, exactly like me and Simon Driscott, although they are way too grown-up for having swivel chair fights!).

We were just now playing *I spy*, but at the moment it is just field, cow, field, cow, field, cow, which is *extreeeeeemely yawn-o-ramic* so we have stopped until we get nearer to London and things get more interesting. I have brought the latest *Hey Girls!* mag with me and we are going to do the quizzes and read the cringes out loud to each other and give them our own star ratings.

So bye for now!

WE ARE HERE!!!

We are in a room called the Green Room, even though it is not actually green. Instead it is a sort of beigy colour and full of free stuff like these woven cake thingies:

Plus, there is coffee and tea and orange juice all ready in jugs that you just pour out. Mum says only one coffee and woven cake thing each or we will be hyper with caffeine and sugar. We are quite hyper-ish already and we keep bursting into giggles about the pure excitement of being about to go on telly!

Oh, hang on...

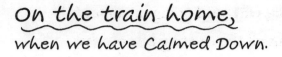

On the train home,
when we have Calmed Down.

We have now Calmed Down. We had to Calm
Down 'cos according to Mum we were being *Too
Silly For Words* and she was threatening to go
and read the paper on her own in the quiet
carriage. I didn't want her to start feeling annoyed
after we've had such a fab day, so we did the
calming down by taking *Deep Cleansing Breaths*
and looking out the window or at mags but not at
each other for at least 8 mins until we stopped
spontaneously exploding into giggles. Plus, I just
reminded Mum about what
Marlene the make-up artist
said and she got so happy
again even just thinking about
it that she walked to the buffet
car on cloud nine and got us all
OJs to celebrate.

Oh hang on, why am I going on about OJs and missing out all the exciting bits of what happened???

I'll pedal backwards to the *start* of what happened, which all began when we got to London. The train ended at Waterloo station and we had to go quite far on the Tube, but actually that was cool 'cos I secretly pretended I was a fashion designer who lived in London and that I was just normally living my everyday life, like travelling on the Tube from my swanky flat to my exclusive boutique.

When we got to the studio, I realized it was that place you sometimes see in the background of *Blue Peter* when they are filming stuff outside. (Not that I watch *Blue Peter now*, obviously. But I did used to when I was a *child*.) There were loads of other buildings round it and it would have been easy to get lost, but luckily a security person helped us find where we were supposed to go.

At the reception we got special passes. We

were meant to hand them back but I accidentally forgot. Well, okay, I *accidentally on purpose* forgot, 'cos I wanted to keep mine as a so~~vener~~ su~~vernir~~ so~~venia~~ souvenir.

I *think* that's right,
hang on, let me ask Tilda – yes, that is right
~~apparently~~ ~~apparently~~ ~~apparetly~~

Hang on again.

apparently

Thanks, T!

So then we were shown to the Green Room which is where I was when I started trying to write in here before. The reason I suddenly had to scribble *hang on* is 'cos someone came in. It was…

Have three guesses.

I've left this space here to give you time to guess

Okay, I will tell you.

It was my ultimate ideal person to arrive —
a hair and make-up artist to get us ready for the
show!

But you say it like
"Mar-lane-a". How
cool is that?!

NAME: MARLENE
JOB: MAKE-UP ARTIST
TV
000058136083519

Marlene is so cool and she had loads of fab make-up
ideas which I am going to try and copy at home,
if Mum helps me. She had this amazing black and pink
hair – like the kind of hair that people would stare at
in Sherborne but that in London is normal and
no one even notices.

Me, Jules and Tilda didn't know we would be
having our make-up professionalistically done so
we got really excited. But also, poor Mum looked a

bit disappointed 'cos her bag was bulging with all the stuff she'd brought, so I was feeling bad for her as well.

We went into *Hair and Make-up*, which was this long thin white room with loads of chair-and-mirror spaces. We changed into our recycled outfits (at last!) and then Marlene put these robe things on us, like the ones you get at the hairdresser, to stop any make-up getting on our clothes, and then we all sat down.

Mum was chatting to Marlene and at first she was shy and just made this tiny suggestion about Tilda's eyeshadow. Then, 'cos Marlene said that was such a good idea, Mum said another bigger suggestion and then showed Marlene all her make-up that she'd brought with her. Then they were both doing us together, and Mum was telling Marlene about her course and Marlene was telling Mum what it's like doing make-up for TV shows all day for your actual **JOB**! (Sounds like the second best job in the world to me – the *best* job is the one I want to have, which is the job of being a *Real Actual Fashion Designer*, of course!)

Gradually we were transformed from quite ordinary schoolgirl-type people into mega-eco-friendly recycled-clothes-wearing babes! It was so cool for Mum too, 'cos Marlene gave her her number and said to call her when she's finished her course 'cos they might be able to give her some work experience at the TV studio. How amazing is that??? Mum was just gobsmackedly going, "Erm, um, er," and then finally she managed to say, "Thank you so much," through her most massivo grin.

Finally we were all made up with our hair done:

We. Looked. Amazing. That is not just me saying so, BTW – I don't want to sound like a massively-big-head. Marlene said this and so did Mum and when Asif the director walked in to see how we were doing he said so too!

NAME: ASIF
JOB: DIRECTOR
TV
0000581399385o

Asif was nice but in a really serious way. He was in charge of everyone and we all just automatically did whatever he told us. Mum said she could do with him at home to get me and Alex into order. Like, ha-ha (not!).

He asked if we felt okay about being in front of the cameras so I just quickly mentioned about how us three have experience in the area of Performing Arts 'cos I went on the catwalk at my own fashion show in aid of charity and at Stella Boyd's show, and 'cos we danced onstage with Jess Moon at the *Hey Girls!* beach party, and about me and Jules modelling in the fashion shoot for the school magazine and how all three of us rocked the Battle of the Bands comp and everything. Asif kept going, "Good, great," so I kept talking, but then I noticed that Mum and Tilda were both doing goggly eyes at me trying to psychically tell me something and that's when I realized that "Good, great," in actual fact meant, *Okay, I get it, now please be quiet*, so I zipped my lips and all was silencio. I felt a bit **CRINGY** about going on and *oooooon*, but on the positive side at least my psychic powers are getting better 'cos it only took me about 24 seconds to work out what Mum and Tilda meant.

Then Tilda said, "I think I'm okay about it...

149

but how many viewers will there be?"

Asif waved his hand to mean *Don't worry* and said, "Oh, probably only about two hundred—"

"Oh, phew, that's okay," said Tilda.

"Thousand," he finished and Tilda went completely paler than she usually is and squeaked, "Two hundred thousand?"

"About that," he said, nodding, not getting that he was totally freaking her out, even though I was doing the goggly eyes thing at him to make him psychically realize. "And then there are the repeats and the showings on our digital channel," he added, making it even worse.

"So no pressure then," said Tilda with a nervous laugh, but she was only half making a joke of it. The other half of her was going, **OH HELP!!!**

Asif went off to talk to the lighting and sound guys and we went back to the Green Room and ate some more woven cake thingies to help with the nerves. In fact, Mum was so nervous for us that instead of saying we couldn't have any more, she had some herself too! Then finally we were called into the studio and all our hearts were pounding, even Jules's, and also we were so trembly that our knees were giving way and we could hardly walk!

Oh, boo! It has been field, cow, field, cow, field, cow for ages now and we are nearly at our stop and Mum is saying, "Right, let's pack our things away and put our litter in the bin," etc. How typical when I am in the middle of telling you about what happened!

Oh, now Mum is saying, "That includes you, Lucy Jessica Hartley," and also, "Stop writing, please."

Oh, now she is taking

That weird ending bit

was Mum confiscating my
fluffy pen, BTW!

Oh, I wish we were still in London! We just
dropped Jules and Tilda off on the way home from
the station. I wanted us to have a celebration tea
together as a three but Mum reckoned there had
been *Enough Excitement For One Day*. That is
another one of her sayings, BTW.

But the good thing is I can carry on telling you
what happened. Well, remember that our hearts
were poundy and our knees were trembly? Luckily,
we managed to walk into the studio on our wobbly
legs by linking arms to hold each other up. And
there, sitting on the sofa thingie, was Aisha, the
presenter! I will just quickly do a pic of her 'cos
I've done one of everyone else so far and it won't
be fair if I don't.

Even though she is famous and could be all sunglasses-wearing and ignoring of us, Aisha was in fact really nice and friendly. I totally loved what she was wearing as well, and I am going to try and copy the top using ribbons and this belt I have.

At first, we all stood there feeling a bit tongue-twisted, but luckily Aisha started mentioning how much she loves our recycled looks and how the room makeover was a really good idea and then we just all started chatting together. Soon I forgot how **FAMOUS** and **AMAZING** she is and I started

seeing her as an actual real person. We talked
about the room makeover and looked at the
photos and explained to her how we'd done
each thing and she said how fab it was. She
showed us where to sit on the couch and said
how we mustn't move about too much or suddenly
lean to the side or we would go out of the shot
and only, say, our elbows and knees
would end up on telly.

Even though we were
actually on set ready to film,
there was still a lot more waiting
while people were

fiddling around with cameras and
lights and stuff. Other people
with clipboards and headphones
kept coming up to talk to Aisha
and we didn't know if we should be
quiet or keep chatting so we just did
waiting and smiling (and I remembered to do my
new smile!).

Then at last Asif was saying, "Okay, everyone, let's go for a take."

Tilda looked really startled and went, "What, like, NOW???" and freaked out, so me and Jules had to put our arms round her in a BFF-type way (but also a *Stop Her Running Off The Set* type way) and I had to say stern things to her like: "Tilda, you will be fine. You are just feeling the high pressures of showbiz, but you have to pull yourself together for the sake of the public. They expect a great performance and we are going to give them one!"

Tilda was just about to say something when Asif came up and showed us to the sides of the stage where we had to come on, and then he shouted "3,2,1 – ACTION!" and Aisha did an intro bit. Then she said about us and Asif gave us a signal and we walked on set and sat on the sofa, and Tilda didn't run away, so my speech must have worked!

Aisha started off by saying, "I'm very excited to

have Lucy, Jules and Tilda with me, to talk about their green project." Then she said how much she liked our recycled outfits, and Jules stood up and did model-y poses while going on and on until Aisha said, "Great. So, Tilda…" and moved it on. So then Jules *had* to sit down, although she did it in slow motion. Tilda didn't say much, but at least she didn't look too terrified. When it was my turn to show my outfit, I found out that the hardest thing was remembering not to look at the camera. In fact, we had to start again a few times because one of us was accidentally staring at it. We were all sitting up very straight and looking very mature, and my voice seemed to have weirdly gone a bit posher, the same as it does when I am talking to Mr. Van der Zwan.

To lead into the room-makeover bit, Aisha said to the camera, "And if you think these girls are amazingly talented now, you'll be even more impressed to hear that they haven't just made these fab recycled fashions, but they've come up with a

156

whole recycled room for Tilda too!" Then she turned back to us three and asked, "How did this come about, girls?" And even though obviously she knew already because we had chatted about it before the filming, she did a really good job of sounding like she didn't.

So I was just about to explain how Mum had been stuck in traffic after the make-up course and about the muesli bar with solid yogurt on that I had to eat and the going to the loo and discovering the vile room and everything, but Tilda got in first. She is so passionate about environmental stuff that she completely forgot her shyness and was talking about all the different elements, like the eco-friendly paint and repainting the furniture, and the recycled rug and everything, while they showed the film of the room. That made me think *Phew* about not mentioning the muesli bar and the going to the loo, etc. 'cos looking back at it I don't think that's what Aisha had meant.

At the end of the interview, Aisha pulled a bag
out from her side of the sofa and went:

I said, "Yeah, sure!" thinking I can design
something when we get home and send her a few
ideas and then if she likes them I can make it for
her. But then she said, "And do you think you
could do it now and then come back and show us
all at the end of the programme?"

So then we were all thinking

YIKES!!!

But of course we had to nod and smile like that was all cool and groovy and not a massively hard challenge!

Oh, gotta go. The phone just went and Mum is calling up the stairs that it's Nan back from Great Auntie Rita's and wanting to know how it went!

Saturday at 11.24 a.m.

I am sooooooo sorry I
didn't get back to writing
in here last night. You must
be totally desperate to
find out what else happened –
especially after Aisha's
shock challenge!

I got distracted yesterday because Nan rang, then
Dad rang, and then I had to help Mum make the
tea because it was getting late, so after that I had
to go in the shower and... Anyway, you
get the picture. At this precise
moment I am supposed to be
entertaining Alex by playing
Monopoly with him. He's
setting it up and I said I'll be
down in one minute so I just have
time to quickly tell you that in the Green Room

we tipped out the bag from Aisha and inside was all this stuff, like:

On TV it will look like we only had about 18 mins to come up with something but in actual fact we had about 45 'cos they were filming this bit about a wormery and the worms kept escaping across the studio (*yurgh!*) and they had to do about 17 takes.

Oh, just a sec…

That was Alex,

saying, "Lucy it has been one minute." I said, "Hang on, I just need 5 more minutes," so he is sitting outside my door counting to sixty, five times. How typical!

Going back to the challenge, we did some quick looking and thinking, and I did some sketches on napkins from the woven-cake table and we made some shorts out of some old jeans, like this:

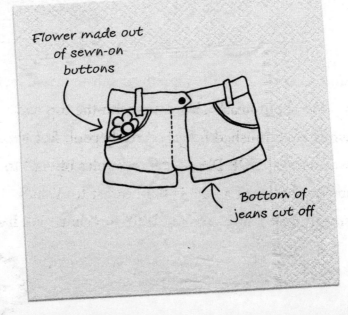

Flower made out of sewn-on buttons

Bottom of jeans cut off

And then we got on with making a top, which was much more complicated 'cos it was like this:

Old black T-shirt cut up

Pink vest top layered over it

This kind of ribbony stuff to hold them together, with beads threaded onto it

We spent nearly all our time on the top and when we'd finished it looked really cool. But then we had a **MAJOR DISASTER** 'cos Jules offered to try on the outfit as she is the nearest to Aisha's size, and the shorts looked **WAY** too short. We had cut them off too high and it was too late to fix them. I was in a total panic and freaking out, going, "Aisha can't wear these! We'll fail the task and look stupid on TV and *everyone* will see and remember it forever!"

Grr, hang on…

<u>Alex just came
in here again,</u> but I have sent him back
downstairs to get us OJ and
Wagon Wheels ready for when
we play the game (clever, huh!).
(BTW, I have found out that Wagon
Wheels are made in Britain and
not the Wild West of America - phew! -
so I am back to eating them again!)

So anyway, as I was saying, I was totally freaking
out, going, "We'll fail the test and look stupid on
TV and my dreams of being a *Real Actual
Fashion Designer* will be over because every
single person in the country of England will
remember this disaster for the entire of **TIME**."

Tilda put her arm round me and said the
speech I'd said to her when *she* was freaking out
back to me, and that made me calm down. And

then Jules said, "Right, let's all think, we need to come up with a new plan...and fast."

Well, can I just stop here and say a big

to my **BFF** for calming me down in a vital moment and saving me from eternal fashion embarrassment. I took some deep breaths and looked at everything again, and then suddenly I was struck with a *Creative Inspiration* to make a skirt like this from the shorts that Jules was still wearing:

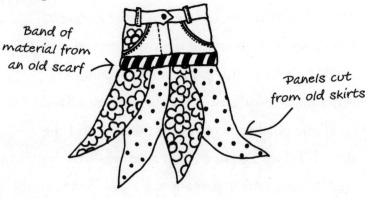

Band of material from an old scarf →

← Panels cut from old skirts

So me and Tilda started madly cutting and sewing and Jules stood there absolutely still in case we accidentally stuck the needle in her leg, going, "This would be easier if I took it off, you know!" but I was like, "There's no time!"

And I was right, because there wasn't even one gazillionth of a moment to spare 'cos the millisecond we finished, Izzy the 2nd AD called us back in. (2nd AD means second assistant director, BTW. She was one of the people at the studio with a clipboard and earpiece thingie who always do what Asif says straight away.)

Oh, ARGH!!!

Excuse me…

Right,

I have now actually paid
Alex in fruit pastilles to stop
bothering me. It cost me
one for every two minutes'
peace, and 'cos I only had
half a packet left I have only
got 14 mins before I HAVE
to play with him. *sigh!*
I will try to write v. v. fast!

Jules quickly changed into her own recycled stuff
and we went back into the studio and we were *all*
nervous about what we'd done and wondering if
Aisha would like it, but especially me, because
fashion designing is the career I want for the rest
of my life, so I really wanted her to love it.

Which, luckily, SHE DID!!!

YAYYYYYYYYYYYYY!!!!!

Asif directed this bit where she whirled around

in her normal clothes and then she changed into the recycled outfit (the skirt did fit – **PHEW!**) and whirled around in that, and the computer tech guys are going to make it look like she is magically changing into our outfit just by the power of whirling (that is *soooooo* the kind of job that Simon Driscott is going to have).

Oh, I have just thought, how cool if you could magically change by simply whirling round in real life? Like, you could be in your uniform at school and if you saw a boy who you liked you could whirl around and suddenly be in your coolest look. Or if you got caught in the rain in a summer dress and ballet pumps you could whirl around and be in jeans and a jacket so you would never have to look like a drowned rat! (Yuck, now I properly think about it that is *such* a horrible saying! I will change it to *so you would never have to look like a sock in a puddle.*)

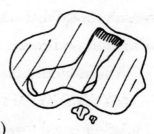

Then we filmed a short bit where Aisha said,
"Wow, did you know you were going to do this
design all along or did it just evolve?" and I said,
"It just evolved," thinking of the too-short-shorts,
and I know Tilda and Jules were thinking the exact
same thing too, 'cos we all started giggling. Asif
shouted, "Cut!" annoyedly and we tried to calm
down and do it again, but we still kept giggling every
time. Even though we were *soooooo* trying not to
we just couldn't help it. We were going, "Sorry,
sorry, sorry," and Aisha was going, "Oh, don't worry
about it, it happens to everyone, we call it corpsing,"
and that was so funny 'cos we were imagining us as
zombies and that made us laugh even more.

We did finally manage to get it done, and then
Asif said it was a wrap and everyone clapped. I
wasn't sure if that was for us or just in general but
I took a bow anyway, just in case.

After we'd finished filming the show, I got
Aisha's autograph which I am sticking in here
for safety.

To Lucy,
You are Fashion Fabulous & a Total Goddess of Green!
Love, Aisha X.

Tilda got her one in an actual autograph book and Jules got hers written on her arm, and she says

she is going to keep it there as long as possible without washing it off. When we were in the studio this guy who was the press

Dear Tilda,
You go girl!
Love Aisha X.

photographer took some pictures of us three together and also of us three with Aisha and, even fabber, he is posting us some. I can't wait for them

to arrive because I have got this top secret surprise
planned for Tilda, which is to blow them up big
and put them in the cool frames we painted on her
walls. That will be just the perfect finishing touch
to her planet-friendly room!

This nice cameraman called Tariq let us see our
TV bits back on the monitor, and there was only
one pair of headphones so we all had to listen
together like this:

I found it completely amazing, 'cos it looked
like we were TV people and not just ordinary. Of
course I had forgotten about doing my mysterious

smile by then and I looked like a toothfully grinning insane person, but never mind.

Mum was so cool 'cos she let us wear our recycled outfits and gorgeous make-up and hair all the way back on the Tube and the train, and we did this fun thing of pretending we were in a girl band when we went to the loo together.

I am *soooooo* massively excited about seeing our bit on the *actual* TV – I wish it was on NOW but Jaime said it will be sometime next spring and they'll write to tell us when exactly. We are getting a DVD of it before then though, when the programme is all put together, so the second we get that, me, Jules and Tilda have already decided that we're having a pizza night to watch it. We're even going to invite Simon Driscott because he helped me with my web research and also he is quite a funny boy and okay when he is not acting like a pillock and making me bash my wrist. Plus, it's Jules's birthday next week and she's having a big *family and friends*

party for it, so we'll probably show it to everyone there too!

I have to go and play with Alex now 'cos my fruit-pastille minutes have run out and he is leaning over me on purpose so I can hardly write in here. I don't really mind 'cos Dad's coming to take him out later (I have double-promised Mum I won't let on that I know about the car-breakdowny date-cringe) and I'm going to meet Jules and Tilda. We're off to the Cool Cats Café for hot chocolate and plus I have to go and choose a new journal from the gifty shop Mum works in 'cos this one has totally run out of pages! After our green project, I'll definitely make sure it is made out of recycled paper, too!

Ow, Alex is poking me! I told him to just let me write one single thing more and then I will play. My one single thing is that I really, really hope you had fun reading about my green designs and that you get inspired to do something green yourself to help save our Planet of Earth.

Lots and lots and lots and lots of love from

Lucy Jessica Hartley x.

(aka the Goddess of Green!!!)

xxx

Don't go yet!
My cool quiz is on
the next page...

Lucy Jessica Hartley's
Planet Fashion Quiz

Are you a Green Goddess or an ENVIRONMENTAL DISASTER?
Find out with my fab eco-quiz!

1. You go to a friend's house and see her throw a whole stack of old mags into the rubbish bin. Do you:

A) Fish them out immediately and show her how easy it is to recycle them instead – there are recycle bins only a couple of streets away after all!

B) Fish them out immediately – there was one you hadn't read yet in that lot! Find it and then throw the rest back in again.

C) Fish them out immediately, and then leave in disgust – how could you hang out with anyone who doesn't recycle their cans, bottles, paper, mags, clothes, shoes and furniture?

2. Which creature is great for turning your old veggie peelings into brand new compost?

A)  B) C)

3. How do you save energy at home?

A) Use low-energy light bulbs and remember to turn them off when you leave the room, oh and switch off the TV at the wall instead of leaving it on standby.

B) Get your little bro to do your drying-up duty for you, and then make him bring you a cup of hot choc afterwards while you curl up on the sofa – that saves loads of energy!

C) Everything in answer A), plus you never turn lights on to get ready, including in the bathroom, even though it means your make-up goes freakily wrong on dark winter mornings, and that you once brushed your teeth with the athlete's-foot cream by mistake.

Mostly As:
Queen of Green!
When it comes to the environment, you know your stuff (well, most of the time!) and you're doing your bit – well done! Now it's time to help your mates go green too!

Mostly Bs:
Hey girl, what planet are you on?!
Kick those bad habits and get the green bug today! Start with simple things like recycling your old mags and you'll soon be on your way to becoming a green goddess!

Mostly Cs:
Eco-worrier!
You're greener than a green thing, but don't let panic about the planet get you down! Volunteer for an eco-project in your area and you'll have fun and make some friends who are as passionate about green issues as you are!

Totally Secret Info about Kelly McKain

Lives: In a small flat in Chiswick, West London, with a fridge full of chocolate.

Life's ambition: To be a showgirl in Paris 100 years ago. *(Erm, not really possible that one! – Ed.)* Okay, then, to be a writer – so I am actually doing it – yay! And also, to go on a flying trapeze.

Star sign: Capricorn (we're meant to be practical).

Fave colour: Purple.

Fave animal: Monkey.

Ideal pet: A purple monkey.

Top green tip: Try growing your own scrummy veggies – even just a few pots on a patio is a good start!

Fave hobbies: Hanging out with my BFF and gorge boyf, watching *Friends*, going to yoga and dance classes, and playing my guitar as badly as Lucy's dad!

Visit Kelly at www.kellymckain.co.uk

Have you read all of Lucy's
hilarious journals?

Makeover Magic

Lucy Jessica Hartley is a style queen, so when
geeky new girl Matilda-Jane starts at school,
she comes up with a fab makeover plan to help
her fit in – and learns a few things about
friendship, too!

ISBN: 9780746066898

Fantasy Fashion

Lucy's fave mag is running a competition to
design a fantasy fashion outfit and Lucy
is determined to win the fab prize –
whatever it takes!

ISBN: 9780746066904

Boy Band Blues

Lucy has been asked to style a boy band for
a Battle of the Bands competition and she's
mega-excited about it – it's just a shame
lead singer Wayne is such a big-head!

ISBN: 9780746066911

Star Struck

Lucy's won a part as a film extra and decides she must get her fab design skills noticed on screen – but will the director appreciate her original efforts?

ISBN: 9780746070611

Picture Perfect

Lucy is in charge of the fashion pages for the school magazine – and she can't wait to get on with the photo shoot! If only she could find a location and some models!

ISBN: 9780746070628

Style School

School fashion guru Lucy sets up a style school in the loos, with lessons in accessories, hair and make-up. But what will happen when the School Uniform Police (aka Mr. Cain) finds out?

ISBN: 9780746070635

Summer Stars

Lucy, Jules and Tilda are off to Newquay on holiday, where their fave mag is holding a beach party! Can they win the dance comp and strut their stuff onstage or will the Greatest Cringe Of All Time crush their dreams of seaside stardom?

ISBN: 9780746080177

catwalk crazy

Lucy is putting on a charity fashion show, but someone seems to be sabotaging all her efforts. Can she track down the culprit and win back her audience before it's too late?

ISBN: 9780746080184

Best Friends Forever

Lucy has decided to makeover the boring school disco into a super-stylish High School Prom. But will she find the right boy to make her big red-carpet entrance with?

ISBN: 9780746080207

check out
www.fiction.usborne.com
for more dazzling
and fabulously funny
girl reads

ALSO BY KELLY MCKAIN

ISBN: 9780746091241

HALF
A SISTER

Hannah is thrilled at the idea of her
newly-discovered half-sister coming
to live with her family. She's always
imagined a lovely sisterly world of
girly chats, swapping make-up and
sharing secrets and clothes.
Beautiful, glamorous Ellie seems to
live up to all Hannah's expectations.
But gradually she begins to realize
that Ellie has a darker side – one that
threatens to tear Hannah's world apart.

**An irresistible, moving tale
of two girls caught up in
a life-changing drama.**

For another fab series full of fun,
friendship, secrets and boys,
check out

SUMMER CAMP SECRETS

by Melissa J. Morgan

MISS MANHATTAN

City chick Natalie is surprised to find that she actually
enjoys summer camp – until her big secret gets out...
ISBN 9780746084557

PRANKSTER QUEEN

Mischievous Jenna is famous for her wild stunts, but this
year she's totally out of control. What's bugging her?
ISBN 9780746084564

BEST FRIENDS?

Fun-loving Grace starts hanging out with Gaby from rival
bunk 3C, before she realizes what a bully Gaby can be.
ISBN 9780746084571

LITTLE MISS NOT-SO-PERFECT

Sporty, reliable Alex seems like the perfect camper. But
she's hiding a problem that she can't bear to admit.
ISBN 9780746084588

BLOGGING BUDDIES

The girls are back home and keeping in touch through their
camp blog. But one bunkmate needs some extra support.
ISBN 9780746084601

PARTY TIME!

Everyone's excited about the camp reunion in New York! But when it gets to party time, will the girls still get on?

ISBN 9780746084618

THREE'S A CROWD

New camper Tori is from LA and is just as super-hip as Natalie. Good thing Nat isn't the jealous type – or is she?

ISBN 9780746093382

WISH YOU WEREN'T HERE

Sarah stresses when classmate Abby turns up at camp – will she expose Sarah as a geek to all her fun-loving friends?

ISBN 9780746093399

JUST FRIENDS?

Priya's best friend is a boy but she's sure she could never have a crush on him – until he starts to like another girl...

ISBN 9780746093405

JUST MY LUCK

When practical jokes start happening during Colour War, Jenna is the obvious suspect. But could someone else be to blame?

ISBN 9780746093412

FALLING IN LIKE

Valerie's wicked stepsister, Tori's forbidden crush, Alyssa's censored artwork...life back home after camp is so complicated!

ISBN 9780746093429

ON THIN ICE

Tori's only allowed to invite five friends on her fab holiday weekend. But how can she choose without hurting anyone?

ISBN 9780746093436

Secrets, hopes, dreams...
These girls share more than just a dorm!
Meet the

School Friends

by Ann Bryant

First Term at Silver Spires

Katy is nervous about going to boarding school for the first
time, especially as she's got a big secret to hide. The girls in
her dorm seem really nice, but when someone sets Katy up
for a fall, how will her new friends react?

ISBN 9780746072240

Drama at Silver Spires

Georgie loves acting and is determined to win her favourite
role in the school play. But her audition goes drastically
wrong when an older girl steals the show instead. Will
Georgie ever get her chance in the limelight now?

ISBN 9780746072257

Rivalry at Silver Spires

Grace is at Silver Spires on a sports scholarship and feels
the pressure to do well in competitions. But when someone
starts writing hurtful messages saying she's just a show-off,
she loses her nerve. Can she still come out on top?

ISBN 9780746072264

Princess at Silver Spires

Naomi hates the attention that comes with people
knowing that she's a princess. But when she's asked to
model in a fashion show, she can't refuse – after all, it's for
her favourite charity...what could go wrong?

ISBN 9780746089576

Secrets at Silver Spires

Jess is really struggling with her lessons. She daren't ask
her friends for help, because she doesn't want them to
find out how stupid she is. But now that she's being made
to go to special classes, how long can she keep her
secret to herself?

ISBN 9780746089583

Star of Silver Spires

Mia's ambition is to be a real musician. She'd love to enter
a song she's written in the Silver Spires Star contest, but
then she'd have to play live onstage too. And performing
in public is her biggest fear ever – can she find the
courage to make her dreams come true?

ISBN 9780746089590

For Sasha Lois,
a future Lucy fan!

First published in the UK in 2008 by Usborne Publishing Ltd., Usborne House, 83-85 Saffron Hill, London EC1N 8RT, England. www.usborne.com

Text copyright © Kelly McKain, 2008.
Illustrations copyright © Usborne Publishing Ltd., 2008

The right of Kelly McKain to be identified as the author of this work has been asserted by her in accordance with the Copyright, Designs and Patents Act, 1988.

Illustrations by Vici Leyhane.

The name Usborne and the devices ♈ ⊕ are Trade Marks of Usborne Publishing Ltd.

A CIP catalogue record for this book is available from the British Library.

ISBN 9780746080191